Praise for *A Christmas by the Sea*

"With a sweet ending that neatly wraps up this Christmas novel, Carlson explores second chances through the touch-ups of a small beach house, a budding romance, and a renewal of faith in God."

Publishers Weekly

"This breezy, entertaining read provides the perfect afternoon getaway during a busy holiday season."

Library Journal

"A Christmas story that will warm your heart and have you dreaming of your own enchanted seaside holiday."

Family Fiction

Praise for *The Christmas Blessing*

"Delightful prose and an affirming resolution will please readers."

Publishers Weekly

"Novelist Melody Carlson has written a deftly crafted, consistently entertaining, and ultimately inspiring story of love, hardship, and reconciliation that will leave readers filled with Christmas joy."

The Midwest Book Review

Praise for *The Christmas Angel Project*

"Carlson's latest holiday offering is sure to become a fan favorite! Full of hope, it embodies all that is beloved about the Christmas season."

RT Book Reviews

Books by Melody Carlson

Christmas at Harrington's
The Christmas Shoppe
The Joy of Christmas
The Treasure of Christmas
The Christmas Pony
A Simple Christmas Wish
The Christmas Cat
The Christmas Joy Ride
The Christmas Angel Project
The Christmas Blessing
A Christmas by the Sea
Christmas in Winter Hill

CHRISTMAS IN
WINTER HILL

MELODY CARLSON

Revell

a division of Baker Publishing Group
Grand Rapids, Michigan

© 2019 by Carlson Management, Inc.

Published by Revell
a division of Baker Publishing Group
PO Box 6287, Grand Rapids, MI 49516-6287
www.revellbooks.com

Printed in the United States of America

Library of Congress Cataloging-in-Publication Data
Names: Carlson, Melody, author.
Title: Christmas in Winter Hill / Melody Carlson.
Description: Grand Rapids, MI : Revell, a division of Baker Publishing Group, [2019]
Identifiers: LCCN 2018052176 | ISBN 9780800736101 (cloth)
Subjects: LCSH: Christmas stories.
Classification: LCC PS3553.A73257 C488 2019 | DDC 813/.54—dc23
LC record available at https://lccn.loc.gov/2018052176

19 20 21 22 23 24 25   7 6 5 4 3 2 1

In keeping with biblical principles of creation stewardship, Baker Publishing Group advocates the responsible use of our natural resources. As a member of the Green Press Initiative, our company uses recycled paper when possible. The text paper of this book is composed in part of post-consumer waste.

 green press INITIATIVE

Krista Galloway didn't usually second-guess herself, but as she slowed down the U-Haul truck on the outskirts of Winter Hill, she was assaulted with some serious doubts. Was this new job a mistake? Should she have researched this move more carefully? Had she agreed to the contract too easily? Too hastily? Being hired as a city manager would definitely improve her résumé, but the small-town salary was a letdown. And what about her daughter's new school? With less than two hundred students, what if its academic standards were disappointing? Why hadn't Krista given this whole thing more consideration?

"Look, Mama!" Emily pointed to the WELCOME TO WINTER HILL billboard. "That sign says HOME OF CHRISTMASVILLE— what does that mean? Does Santa Claus live here?" Emily giggled like she knew better.

"What do you think?" Krista grimaced at the plywood Christmas tree alongside the welcome sign. It could use a new coat of paint.

"I know, Santa isn't really real. But are we near the North

Pole now? You said it snowed a lot here." Emily peered eagerly out the window, almost as if she expected to see snowflakes flying.

"It does snow here," Krista confirmed. "But it's still late autumn, Emily." She pointed to where some orange and gold leaves still clung to a large tree, vibrating in the afternoon breeze.

"But why did that sign say HOME OF CHRISTMASVILLE?" Emily persisted.

"I'm not sure." Krista vaguely remembered someone mentioning a Christmas festival during her second Skype interview with the hiring committee, but she'd been so caught up in impressing them that she'd barely registered the information. And, naturally, she didn't admit that she had a general aversion to Christmas. What did that have to do with managing a small town anyway?

"Where *is* Christmasville? What is it?"

Krista felt a mixture of amusement and aggravation at her eight-year-old's dogged determination. Her little apple hadn't fallen far from the tree when it came to questioning things.

"I'm not completely sure what Christmasville is," Krista admitted as she drove past a suburb on the edge of town. "But I do know that Winter Hill has an annual Christmas festival. That must be what Christmasville is. I suppose it could be related to the town's name."

"Winter Hill," Emily said dreamily. "That does sound like a Christmassy place. I'm so glad we're moving here."

Krista turned the bulky truck onto a quiet side street, pausing to check the little hand-drawn map that Pauline Harris, a city assistant, had mailed her last week, along with a brass key. "It looks like our house is only a few blocks from here," she told Emily. "We're almost home."

"We get to live in a *real* house," Emily happily declared. "With a *real* backyard. And when it snows—because you said it'll snow—I can go outside and make a *real* snowman."

"This is going to be very different from Arizona." Krista hadn't been sorry to leave Phoenix or their high-rise apartment behind. Really, she was ready for a change. And although Winter Hill was very small, Krista was glad that Emily could walk to school from their house. Pauline had assured Krista that it was only three blocks away—with crossing guards. Not only that, but Krista could walk to work too. Perfect since she hadn't owned a car for the last five years.

Like Emily, Krista was looking forward to a new life in the quaint eastern Washington town. She'd never lived anywhere but Phoenix, and the idea of snow and seasons was rather exciting. Krista slowed down the truck, looking for the right address. But seeing the numerals on a small sign in front of what appeared to be an apartment complex was not encouraging. Krista pulled over with a disappointed sigh.

"What's wrong, Mama?"

She pointed at the dismal concrete building. "I think that's our new home."

Emily leaned over to see it better. "It's not a house?"

"Looks like it's an apartment." Krista surveyed the concrete one-story complex, trying to insert some hopefulness into her voice. "But it's not very big. It looks like only about a dozen units. That's sort of like a house." She picked up the map that Pauline had mailed, noticing that next to the address was another number. "I think we must be in unit eight."

"Eight?" Emily's mouth twisted to one side. "Well, that's a good number. I'm eight too. Maybe it won't be so bad."

"Maybe not." Krista eased the big truck into the parking

spot in front of unit eight, relieved to be finally done with this grueling journey. "At least we won't have to lug our stuff up a bunch of stairs." She turned off the engine. "Hopefully we can get the truck unloaded before dark and sleep in our own beds tonight." She stepped outside the truck and stretched. After two nights in cheap roadside motels, she would welcome her own bed and nice sheets tonight.

"It's cold." Emily shivered with wide eyes. "Do you think it's going to snow?"

"I don't know. Why don't you put on your new parka?" Krista reached for her phone, searching for the number Pauline had told her to text upon arrival. Apparently Pauline's son had promised to be available to help unload the U-Haul. Krista shot off a text then held up the brass key. "Ready to see our new home?" She tried to sound more enthused than she felt as she led the way to the apartment.

Pauline Harris had told Krista that available housing was an issue in Winter Hill. "That's because people keep moving here from California," she'd explained, promising to find something within Krista's budget and near the grade school. But for some reason, when Pauline had sent the key and brief description of the small two-bedroom abode, Krista had assumed it was a house. She slid the key into the lock then opened the door.

"Welcome home," she said brightly, trying not to frown at the stark white walls and dingy beige carpet. "I'm sure it'll look better when we get our things in here." She went through the living room into the compact kitchen and flipped on the overhead light to see shabby wood cabinets, mismatched appliances, and plastic countertops. Nothing like their sleek, modern Phoenix apartment with granite and stainless. Well, hopefully they wouldn't be stuck here for too long. Although she regretted the six-month lease she'd signed.

"Which is my room?" Emily called from down the hallway.

Krista joined her to discover two identical bedrooms with a clean but dull-looking bathroom between them. "I don't know." She pursed her lips, trying to disguise her dismay. "You choose, honey."

Emily ran from room to room, finally deciding. "I can see big trees from this window," she declared. "Do you think they're in our backyard?"

Krista wondered if they even had a backyard but then remembered a door in the kitchen. "Let's go find out." She was disappointed to find the door opened to a windowless laundry room. Although appliances were in place, they were probably older than she was. Hopefully they worked.

Krista wrapped an arm around Emily. "Well, we'll just have to consider this a big adventure." She gave her a squeeze. "We will make the best of it."

"Hello?" a male voice called out. "Help has arrived."

"That must be Pauline's boy." Krista returned to the living room, expecting to find a teenager. But there was a man standing in the open doorway. Tall and sturdy looking, he wore jeans and a flannel shirt and was smiling. "Who are you?" she asked cautiously.

"I'm Conner Harris." His dark eyes brightened as he stuck out his hand. "My mom is Pauline Harris. You just texted me that—"

"Yes, yes." Krista shook his hand. "I'm Krista Galloway. For some reason I thought you'd be a kid. I mean Pauline said her *boy* would help me and I just assumed you'd—"

"Yes, I'll always be my mom's little boy." He chuckled, then smiled at Emily. "And who is this young lady?"

"I'm Emily Galloway." She politely extended her hand.

"It's a pleasure to meet you, Emily Galloway." He nodded toward the front door. "My daughter, Anna, is out there."

"Is she my size?" Emily's eyes lit up. She'd been obsessed with the idea of making new friends these past few days.

"Not anymore." Conner sighed. "Anna's fourteen now, but it seems like just yesterday she was your size."

"Fourteen?" Emily's eyes grew wide. "That's old."

"Anyway, we're here to help." He smiled at Krista. "Ready to get started?"

"Yes, I'm hoping to get it all unloaded before dark. We don't have a lot of stuff. But some of it is bulky."

As they went outside, a slender girl with thick dark hair and brown eyes climbed out of a big white pickup. "This is Anna." Conner introduced the rest of them. Anna shyly greeted them, staying close to her father. "She might look delicate, but believe me, she's strong as a horse."

"You're pretty." Emily took Anna's hand. "I like your tennis shoes."

Anna glanced down at her red high-topped Converse shoes then smiled. "Thanks. They're kind of old and beat up, but I like them too."

"Do you wanna see my room?" Emily asked hopefully.

"Sure." Anna nodded.

"Good idea," Conner told Anna. "You go check out the lay of the land, and we'll put together a plan for unloading."

Before long, with Conner directing, all four of them were busily carrying furnishings, boxes, and bags into the apartment, trying to get the larger pieces into the right rooms. "It's a good thing we don't have too much stuff," Krista told him as the last load came in. "We wouldn't have room for it in this place."

"My mom was sorry she couldn't find you guys better accommodations," Conner said. "But good housing is scarce these days."

"Yes, I understand the town is growing." Krista pushed a strand of golden hair away from her eyes. She could hear the girls chattering in Emily's bedroom. It sounded like Anna was helping Emily make her bed. "That's probably why they decided to hire a city manager."

"I must admit that I'm surprised they hired such a young one." Conner studied her. "Have you had much experience?"

Krista stood up straighter, looking him directly in the eyes and realizing he was nearly a foot taller than her. Just one challenge of being petite. The biggest challenge was being treated like a child by some people. But she was used to it. "Apparently the hiring committee felt my experience was adequate. I went to work for the City of Phoenix straight out of college. After seven years, I was appointed to assist the city manager. I held the assistant position these past three years. And, in case you haven't heard, Phoenix has a population of more than one and a half million. It was a fairly demanding job, but I learned a lot."

"Well, that does sound impressive. I guess Winter Hill was lucky to get you." He looked amused. "And I hope you and Emily are happy here in our little town."

"Dad?" Anna called from Emily's room. "Can they come to the house moving with us?"

"House moving?" Krista frowned. "What's that?"

"We're relocating an old house to a new location," he explained. "It has to be done on a Sunday evening because there's less traffic." He checked his watch. "We're scheduled to start the move in about half an hour. And I need to be there."

"You're moving a house?" she asked. "A *whole* house?"

"I'm not actually moving it myself," he told her. "A moving crew is handling it. I just need to supervise."

Emily came out, tugging on Krista's arm. "Can we go see it? Anna said it's a Christmas House." Emily looked up with wide-eyed enthusiasm. "Please, Mama. I've never seen a Christmas House before."

"And I've never seen anyone move a house before," Krista admitted. "It sounds like fun."

"Then let's go." Conner pulled out his keys. "I promised Anna we'd swing by Comet's Drive-In to grab something to eat while we watch. You ladies care to join us for dinner and a show?"

As Emily jumped up and down, squealing with delight, Krista turned to Conner. "It does sound like fun, but I need to turn in the U-Haul truck before they close—"

"That's right down the street from Comet's," he told her. "We can meet up with you there." He explained that the U-Haul place would already be closed, but that she could park the truck and put the keys into a drop box by the door. "Just follow me and we'll pick you up there."

It took less than ten minutes to drop off the truck. Then Krista and Emily climbed into Conner's big white pickup. "Emily can sit with me." Anna helped Emily into the back.

"Your truck is awesome," Emily declared sweetly. "Lots nicer than our moving truck. And it even has a backseat. Your family is lucky."

As Krista fastened her seat belt, she wondered about Anna's mother . . . Conner's wife. She'd discreetly observed the plain gold band on Conner's left hand. What would Mrs. Harris think of him taking a divorcée and her daughter to "dinner and a show"? Not that this was a date—it certainly was not—but some wives could get rather irate over something like this. Krista had been upset when her husband had stepped out with another woman several years ago. Of course, that was different. This was perfectly innocent. It was silly to even think like that.

As Conner pulled into a brightly lit drive-in restaurant that looked straight out of an old fifties movie, Krista bristled at being reminded of her ex just now. Why give him a second thought? Garth Galloway, currently living a carefree life with his new wife on the other side of the country, didn't deserve that kind of attention.

2

omet's Drive-In wasn't only cute as can be, it was fast. When the waitress brought out their to-go orders in brown paper bags, Krista suddenly grew ravenous. She sniffed the bag in her lap. "Something smells delicious."

"I don't think you'll be disappointed." Conner backed out of the drive-in space.

"This place is awesome," Emily declared. "I wish we had a car, Mama. We could come and eat like those people. See the tray on their car. That's so cool."

"We'll have a car soon," Krista assured her, wishing she'd taken care of this before they'd moved. Sure, they could walk a lot of places, but there was no metro like in Phoenix. And although they'd brought bicycles, biking wouldn't be practical with a foot of snow on the ground. Would they need snowshoes? Krista had never experienced snow and had no idea what to expect.

Within minutes, Conner parked his pickup on the blocked-off street and they all sat down on a folded blanket laid over the open tailgate. Krista felt like a kid as she kicked her feet back and forth, eating the best burger, fries, and shake ever, while watching the procession of heavy equipment operators—tractors, trucks, and trailers—all working together to meticulously extract the small cottage from the lot.

"That house has been there for more than a hundred years," Conner explained. "But it's built solid as a rock. I just hope nothing cracks up too much by the time they get it across town."

"Where are they taking it?" Emily asked.

"Not too far from your apartment," he told her. "Just the other side of the grade school."

"Why is it being moved?" Krista took another bite.

"This property is being developed for new homes," he explained.

"Dad is building them," Anna said proudly.

"Not by myself," he said quietly. "I have a good crew. We plan to put up twenty small houses in here. Affordable houses. But attractive and with quality construction."

"Well, this town needs housing." Krista reached for her milkshake. "Looks like you're doing your part. But wouldn't it have been easier to tear the cottage down? And cheaper?"

"Maybe," he conceded. "But it's kind of a special little house."

"It was built by the founding family of Winter Hill," Anna told them. "Dad wanted to preserve it."

"But I still don't know why it's called the *Christmas House*." Emily took a big bite of her burger.

"The Christmas House?" Krista asked.

"That's right," Conner said. "That's what we're calling it."

"But why?" Emily asked.

"Because it's part of our Christmas celebration," Anna patiently explained. "Have you heard about Christmasville, Emily?"

"I saw that on the sign," Emily said with a full mouth. "What is it?"

"Chew your food before you talk," Krista quietly reminded her.

"Winter Hill is famous for Christmasville," Anna said. "Trust me, you're going to absolutely love it."

"What's it like? What happens at Christmasville?" Emily asked.

"All sorts of things. The whole town helps put it together," Anna said. "We build this whole Christmas town. There's the Santa Claus house, and Santa's workshop, and Mrs. Claus's kitchen, and a candy shop, and a toy shop, and we even have an ice rink and—"

"There she goes." Conner pointed to the house, which was now solidly on the street and starting to move a bit more quickly. "I want to follow it down the street." He slid off the tailgate.

"Can Emily and I stay back here?" Anna asked him.

"Well, I don't know." Conner glanced at Krista. "I'd let Anna sit back here since we'll only go about five miles an hour, but you might not want Emily to ride—"

"Please, Mama, *please!*"

"Only five miles an hour?" Krista questioned.

"Yes. If we need to go any faster, we could have the girls get in the cab."

"Please," Emily pleaded.

"Will you be really, really careful?" Krista asked her.

"I'll watch Emily," Anna assured Krista. "I'll make sure she's safe."

"I'll do whatever Anna tells me," Emily said. *"Please."*

"Well, five miles an hour is about like a fast walk," Krista conceded. "I suppose it's okay." She zipped Emily's parka the rest of the way up then shook her finger at her. "Be safe and stay warm."

"We'll wrap up in the blanket," Anna said as Conner helped Krista down, then closed the tailgate. Soon they were back in the cab, and keeping a safe distance, Conner followed the house. It traveled like a giant, well-lit snail as it advanced down the street. Although it was dark, a number of interested onlookers lined the street, calling out greetings as the slow-moving processional passed by.

"This feels kind of like a nighttime parade." Krista polished off the last bite of her burger. "Fun."

"Too bad I didn't think to add some green lights to the house. And I could've put on some Christmas music. I didn't realize spectators would come out to watch the move." He waved to a woman with a camera. "That's Beth Seymour," he told Krista. "She works for the newspaper. I'll bet the Christmas House makes the front page of Wednesday's edition. But that's because we're such a small town there's never any really big news."

The woman with the camera waved back as she ran over to the pickup. "Hey, Conner," she called into the cab. "Can I hitch a ride with you?"

"Sure." He slowed to a stop then climbed out. "Hop in." He pushed up the console dividing the seats, helping Beth to get in and pausing to introduce the two women.

"So you're the new city manager." Beth shook Krista's hand

with enthusiasm. "Maybe I can get some photos of you too. This is great. Killing two birds with one stone." She glanced over her shoulder. "Who's that back there with Anna?"

"That's my daughter, Emily." Krista explained that they'd just arrived and that Conner and Anna had helped them move in. "This is the first we've seen of town."

"See that building over there?" Beth pointed to a three-story brick building. "That's City Hall. Where you'll be working."

"That's a big building for a small town."

"Well, City Hall is on the top floor. The library is on the second floor. And the first floor, which used to house the police station, is now used for office space, although much of it is unoccupied. But I hear it will be put to good use for Christmasville this year."

"Interesting." Krista asked a few more questions and, as the pickup crept along, Beth continued giving her the lowdown on other points of interest.

"Beth is a great resource in this town," Conner said as they stopped to wait for the house to turn a corner. "She knows everyone and everything."

As the processional picked up speed again, still creeping along at five miles an hour, Krista felt uneasy. She'd nearly forgotten that she'd planned for Emily to go to school in the morning. "How long do you think it'll take to get the house completely moved and situated?"

"It's about three more blocks," he told her. "Shouldn't be too long."

"And that's the grade school up ahead." Beth pointed to a single-story brick structure. "I'm guessing your daughter will go there."

"That's right." Krista nodded. "Do you know much about the school?"

"Both my sons attended there. I believe we have some of the best teachers in the state. Honestly, I can only sing their praises. My boys are in middle school now . . . that's another story. But from what I hear most middle schools are like that."

"Anna would concur with you," Conner said. "She's been much happier in high school."

"That's a relief." Beth pointed to a pretty Victorian house on a corner. "We're just entering the historical neighborhood now."

"That's where we're putting the Christmas House," Conner told Krista. "An old house was so badly neglected and full of dry rot, it had to be bulldozed. But that left a lovely little lot for the Christmas House, and Mayor Richards talked the owner into donating it as a tax write-off."

"It helped that the owner was Mayor Richards' mother-in-law," Beth explained, "so it wasn't too difficult to talk her into it."

Krista laughed. "Already, I'm feeling like I really do live in a small town—and I like it."

"Where did you move from?" Beth asked.

"Phoenix."

Beth began to interview Krista, asking professional as well as personal questions, and by the time the house was being eased onto the readied lot, she appeared to have accumulated enough information for a fairly comprehensive article.

"You really did kill two birds with one stone," Krista told Beth as Anna and Emily got back into the cab to watch the house getting settled onto its new foundation.

"It was pretty cold out there," Emily said.

"I'll give you my coat." Krista started to pull off her jacket.

"That's okay," Anna told her. "We've got an extra blanket. I'll wrap her up in it."

"Is it going to snow tonight?" Emily asked.

Conner laughed. "I hope not. No snow in this week's forecast. Although we've had snow before Thanksgiving in the past."

"One time we had snow on Halloween," Anna said. "Trick-or-treating was no fun that year."

"I've never seen snow before at all—not ever," Emily said longingly. "And I thought we were gonna have a real backyard here, and I wanted to build a real snowman. But our apartment doesn't have any yard."

"Maybe you'll win the Christmas House," Anna told her.

"Win a house?" Emily asked with wonder. "How do you win a house?"

"It's part of the Christmasville celebration," Beth explained. "The city is going to give away the house."

"The *whole* house?" Emily asked. "For real?"

"Is it a raffle?" Krista asked.

"No, it's a contest," Beth explained. "People are invited to write essays."

"What's an essay?" Emily asked.

"It's like a story," Anna said.

"It's all in the newspaper. We've been covering all the details and how to submit it." She pointed out the window to where the men were working on the house. "But I need to get some photos of this."

"And I need to check on something." Conner opened the door.

Before getting out, Beth turned to Krista. "I've enjoyed

meeting you. Do you mind if I call you tomorrow? I'd like to get a good photo of you for this week's paper. And I have some more questions."

"That'd be great." Krista smiled. "Just call City Hall and ask for me."

Beth promised to do that, then she and Conner hurried over to get a better look at the house-moving operation.

"I wish I could win that house," Emily said wistfully.

Krista checked her watch. "You know, tomorrow is a school day." She turned to look at Emily. "And it's past your bedtime." She looked at Anna. "And I'm sure your dad has more things to attend to here. But our apartment is only a few blocks away. I think Emily and I should just walk home." She asked Anna to thank her dad and explain their need to go home and then they left.

Krista held Emily's hand as they hurriedly walked the few blocks, going past the school, and finally arriving at the apartment. "It really is cold here," Krista admitted as she unlocked the door. "We might need to get even more winter clothes." She'd ordered a few things online in Phoenix, but suddenly the idea of long underwear was extremely appealing.

"It's cold, but I like it." Emily sounded tired as they went inside. "I *love* Winter Hill and I love our new friends. And I can't wait until Christmasville. I'm really, really glad we came here, Mama. This really is a big adventure, isn't it?"

Krista agreed that it was an adventure as she helped Emily get ready for bed. Tucking her in with some extra blankets and wondering if the heating system in the apartment even worked, Krista tried to reflect her daughter's enthusiasm for their new life in Winter Hill. And she spoke positively about the new school Emily would be enrolled in tomorrow. But as she listened to Emily's bedtime prayer, Krista felt a stab to her heart.

"Please, dear God," Emily prayed after asking God to bless all their newly made friends, "please, please, let us win the Christmas House. We really need a house like that. A real house. Please, help us to win it. Thank you. Amen."

Krista had to hold her peace as she kissed Emily good night. She didn't want to thwart her daughter's childlike faith, but she didn't like that Emily had asked God to give them the Christmas House. A prayer like that could only lead to disappointment. Krista had experienced plenty of that kind of disillusionment when she was Emily's age. Somehow she would have to gently discourage her daughter, to lovingly prepare her for the reality that not all prayers get answered . . . not all dreams come true.

Krista tried not to think about her own dismal childhood as she paced back and forth in the plain and overly crowded apartment. Abandoned shortly after her birth but not "adoptable," she'd lived in numerous foster homes. Some good, some not so much. She tweaked the thermostat again, turning it up to ninety degrees in hopes that it would take the chill off the place, then started to unpack the kitchen boxes.

By the time the lackluster kitchen was somewhat organized, the heating system was finally starting to work. Unfortunately, the warmth radiated from the ceiling—her head was warm, but her feet were like ice. The idea of spending the whole winter in a cold and uncomfortable apartment was disturbing. And six months here? That was downright depressing!

Maybe this wasn't such a great idea after all. Besides their disappointing new abode, there was another thought nagging at her. Why hadn't she done more thorough research? With the various places seeking a city manager, why had she settled so quickly and easily for the one town that appeared to be eternally linked to Christmas?

Krista pushed a pile of linens aside and, sitting in the corner of her sofa, pulled her chilled feet underneath her and attempted to face her demons. Her Christmas demons. Had she always hated Christmas? She tried to remember a time when she had enjoyed the celebration. But her earliest holiday memories were filled with disappointment after disappointment. It hadn't helped that her birthday was on Christmas Eve. That was like a double whammy. Not only did her expectations for Christmas get dashed, her birthday was usually forgotten as well. Not much fun for a child.

By the time she was twelve, Krista pretended to be Jewish around her friends. It was a simple solution for avoiding Christmas altogether. But at fifteen she discovered her own genuine faith at a Christian youth group camp that her foster family had sent her to—probably just to be rid of her for a couple of weeks. After that, although she could celebrate the *idea* of Jesus' birthday, she soon learned that history suggested the December 25 date was probably erroneous. It figured. And she secretly suspected that Jesus probably wasn't a big fan of all the hullabaloo and commercialism that surrounded the rather confusing holiday either.

Unfortunately, her Christmas memories didn't improve much in adulthood. Sometimes she wondered if she'd somehow attracted these disappointments—like a seasonal curse. One year, she'd been in a car wreck at Christmastime. Another year she'd had a horrible case of flu. When she and Garth married she'd been relieved to learn that he wasn't overly fond of

Christmas either. And when Emily came along, they kept it low-key . . . until she began to ask for more.

But then, when Emily was five, Krista had discovered that Garth was having an affair . . . just days before Christmas. A year later, at Christmastime, their divorce was finalized. And last Christmas, just one year ago, Garth had remarried. Now she was going to live in Christmasville. Merry Christmas.

· 3 ·

Krista's frame of mind was somewhat improved in the morning. A relatively good night's sleep in her own bed, followed by pancakes, canned applesauce, and Emily's brightly shining face, bolstered her spirits. Maybe this move hadn't been a mistake.

"I'm sorry we don't have milk or eggs," Krista said as she rinsed their dishes. "I'll pick some things up after work today."

"What time do you get done with your work, Mama?"

"Five o'clock." Krista forced a smile. She hated that Emily had to endure such long days, but this was how it had always been. Emily was used to it. "Remember I told you that there's an after-school program at your school—I'll pick you up there. Probably by five-thirty at the latest."

Emily peered out the living room window as she tugged on her parka. "It didn't snow yet."

"Be patient. I'm sure it will come." Krista checked herself in the mirror still leaning against the wall by the front door. She'd worn her best business suit—a dark teal blue that she'd been told brought out the color of her eyes. She smoothed her hair, which she'd pinned into a tight French twist. Her natural color was what she'd always called "dirty blonde," but her hairdresser claimed was really "honey-gold." Maybe . . . after highlights were added. Although they only showed up when her mid-length hair fell loose over her shoulders. For today's first impression, she didn't care about highlights. She wanted to look buttoned-up and professional. She'd even packed her fake dark-rimmed glasses in her faux Birkin bag. Just in case. As a petite younger woman, she'd learned long ago that she needed to present herself as authoritative and capable. Hopefully she'd be able to lighten up her appearance later on down the line.

Krista pulled on the long black wool coat she'd purchased online. "It's so strange to wear these winter coats." She wrapped a soft blue scarf around her neck. "So different from Phoenix."

"I like it." Emily tugged on her new mittens. "It's like living in a picture book. All we need is the snow."

Krista chuckled at the mittens as she helped Emily with her backpack. "I'll bet the day will come when you'll be sick of snow, honey."

"No way." Emily firmly shook her head.

"You'll have to eat the school lunch today," Krista told Emily as they went outside, where the sun was shining brightly but the air was crisp and cold. "And we won't always have to walk everywhere. I'll look into getting us a car. As soon as I can."

"If we get a car, we can go to Comet's," Emily declared.

They chatted pleasantly as they walked, Emily pointing out each new point of interest along the way, until the school came into sight.

Krista studied the older building, wondering what it would feel like to go to such a small school. Emily's old school had more than six hundred students. "Well, here it is. Roosevelt Elementary School. What do you think, Em?"

"I like it." But she looked slightly nervous. "I just hope I make a friend today. I've been praying for a BFF. Kind of like Olivia back in Phoenix. But she never was a *real* BFF. Sometimes she was mean."

"Well, I'm sure you'll make plenty of friends here," Krista assured her. "But remember a best friend takes time." Krista didn't want to admit—not yet anyway—that she'd never had a real BFF herself.

As they followed the sign pointing to the administration office, Krista didn't see any visible security. There'd been no guard at the door, no one checking bags.

"I'm surprised you don't have more security," Krista said to the receptionist as she signed in at the front desk.

The receptionist laughed. "In a town this small? Trust me, everyone knows everyone here. If I noticed anything out of order, we'd have the police here in two minutes. The station is only four blocks away."

"Oh." Krista nodded. "That sounds pretty secure."

The receptionist directed Krista and Emily to Principal Richards' office, where they were met by a gray-haired woman with kind gray eyes.

"Welcome to Roosevelt," she told Emily. "Miss Willis is our third grade teacher. I think you'll like her." Then, as an office helper escorted Emily to her classroom, Krista filled out the necessary paperwork and signed some forms.

"Emily's records are already in our system," Mrs. Richards said as Krista handed her the paperwork. "I hope you and Emily will like our little town."

"We only arrived yesterday, but we already like it." Krista explained about watching the house moving last night. "It was a charming snippet of small-town life."

"Wasn't that exciting!" Mrs. Richards' eyes lit up. "My husband and I watched the whole thing."

Krista suddenly remembered something. "Isn't the mayor's name Richards too? Is he related to you?"

"Yes. That's my husband, Barry. You'll probably meet him today."

"So it was your family that donated the lot for the Christmas House."

She nodded. "It's such a fun little project. We all love Christmasville, and the house contest makes it even more exciting this year."

"I've been hearing a lot about Christmasville. It sounds like a big event."

"Oh, yes. The biggest event of the year." She chuckled. "And don't tell Emily this, but Barry and I have a special role during Christmasville." She lowered her voice. "Mr. and Mrs. Claus."

"Really?" Krista feigned enthusiasm. "That must be fun."

"We're not the only ones playing Santa. Several of us old-timers don the costumes. But Barry and I have the privilege of performing our roles during the parade as well as opening night of Christmasville."

"Opening night?"

"Yes. It's always on the Saturday after Thanksgiving. The parade is early in the day and the opening night is the same evening. Then Christmasville is open right up until Christmas Eve, when we have another big celebration. Oh, it's a busy time, but so worthwhile. The children absolutely love it. Well, everyone does."

Krista glanced at the calendar behind Mrs. Richards' desk. "So . . . the Christmasville opening is less than two weeks away."

"A very busy two weeks. Which probably means you'll have a lot to do as our new city manager." Mrs. Richards checked her watch. "Now, don't let me keep you from getting over to City Hall. I'm sure everyone there is excitedly awaiting your arrival." She patted Krista on the shoulder. "And don't worry about Emily, I'm sure she'll be just fine. We've already assigned her an elf buddy."

"An *elf buddy*?"

"That's a classmate who will help Emily find her way around the school and fit into our routines." Mrs. Richards winked. "Laurel Myers is an absolute darling."

"Oh, that's nice to hear." Krista thanked her and, feeling assured of Emily's welfare, excused herself. Hopefully she'd fare as well at City Hall. Maybe they would assign her an elf buddy too.

As Krista walked the few blocks to City Hall, she was impressed by the quaint town. Old-fashioned buildings, iron lampposts, sidewalks paved like cobblestones. It was absolutely charming. Like Emily had said earlier, it was similar to a picture book. And she could see how this town would easily lend itself to a celebration like Christmasville. Naturally, this only made her earlier apprehensions return. Perhaps she really was the wrong choice for this job.

And if Principal Richards' insinuations were correct about Krista's role as city manager, some other things were starting to make sense. After the position had been offered to her in late October, Krista had suggested she step into the position *after* the New Year. But the committee had insisted she give her notice to the City of Phoenix and make the transition as quickly as possible. The eagerness of the committee now suggested Krista might have responsibilities for Christmasville.

But was that fair? Was it ethical to expect a city manager to deal with an event that obviously took place in off-hours and outside of the workplace?

The first thing Krista noticed on the City Hall building was how the windows of the first floor were covered in red and green paper with colorful signs stating FUTURE HOME OF CHRISTMASVILLE. Of course, there was also a smaller sign saying OFFICE SPACE FOR LEASE. It appeared the city had their priorities firmly set. Christmasville was more important than potential city revenue. Interesting.

As she rode the elevator to the third floor, Krista considered the contract she'd signed a few weeks ago. Nothing had appeared out of the ordinary. In fact, it had been a rather simple and straightforward agreement. According to her job description, she'd be doing the usual things—supervising day-to-day operations of city departments, overseeing staff and department heads. She'd have some responsibilities over the city budget and act as advisor to the city council and mayor, as well as a liaison with Winter Hill citizens. Normal expectations for a small-town city manager. Nothing in the contract had assigned, described, or attached any city managerial responsibilities to Christmasville. She would have noticed that!

As Krista stepped out of the elevator, an older woman greeted her. "You must be Krista Galloway." She stuck out her hand with a wide smile. "I'm Pauline Harris—your assistant."

Krista shook her hand, unsure how she felt about having an older woman for an assistant. "I'm pleased to meet you, Ms. Harris."

"Oh, please, call me Pauline. After all, we'll be working closely together."

"Thank you." Krista resisted the urge to have Pauline call

her by her first name. Not yet anyway. Not until she established herself here.

"Did you get moved in okay?" Pauline led her over to the reception area.

"Yes. Thank you for sending your son and granddaughter to help us. We couldn't have done it without them. They took us to see the house moving. Quite an evening." She unbuttoned her coat and unwound her scarf.

"Oh, wasn't that fun? I was there too. For part of it anyway. But it got so cold, I left early. I assume it all got put into place okay. Otherwise, I'm sure we'd have heard something by now."

"Hello, hello." A round-faced man with curly gray hair approached them.

"This is Mayor Richards," Pauline told Krista.

"Pleased to meet you, Ms. Galloway." The mayor frowned ever so slightly as he shook her hand. "But . . . you're younger than I recalled."

She forced a smile, giving him a brief yet impressive description of her experience. "Although I suspect the City of Phoenix's challenges are more complicated than Winter Hill's, I believe working side by side with a city manager of such a large cosmopolitan metropolis was excellent training ground for me. Besides my work experience, my bachelor's degree is in business management and my master's is in public administration—and I don't like to brag, but I graduated in the top ten percent of my class."

"Well, then I'm sure we're fortunate to have you, Ms. Galloway. Welcome aboard." He turned to Pauline. "Are we still meeting at ten?"

She nodded. "Yes. I was just printing out the agenda. Would you like to give Ms. Galloway the two-bit tour?"

"Be glad to."

"Why don't I take your coat and things," Pauline offered. Krista handed them off to her.

"And we'll catch up with you in the conference room." He nodded toward a nearby hall. "How about if we get some coffee first?" He led her to the staff room where she met a couple of employees and the mayor presented her with a cup of coffee in a Christmasville mug—of course!

As they strolled along, the mayor slowed down to point out various photos and posters displayed along the walls. Most were related to Christmasville. He also paused to introduce her to various city employees, including a custodian and a pair of outdoor maintenance men. Then he took her down to the second floor. As he showed her a large display outside the library, depicting the history of Christmasville, which was celebrating its tenth year, she told him about meeting his wife at the school. "She was a lovely person. I know my little girl is in good hands."

"Yes, Lydia is a saint. Never saw anyone who loves kids like her." He winked at her. "Probably why she makes such a good Mrs. Claus."

"And I hear you are *Mr.* Claus," Krista said.

"Yes. Lydia had to twist my arm at first. But we've been doing it for the past ten years and it's turned into a most enjoyable privilege."

"It sounds as if the whole town gets into the act."

"Oh, yes. It takes a village to raise a Christmasville." He chortled as they rode the elevator back up. "But it's a lot of fun." As they emerged on the third floor, he paused to introduce her to a man in a sharp-looking dark suit. "This is Byron Peters, our city attorney. His office is down on the first floor. That's where the police station used to be, but they just relocated to a new building over on Fifth Street."

"So far, it's only me down in the lonely, deserted dungeon," the attorney told her.

"I noticed it appeared primarily vacant," she said.

"Not for long," the mayor assured her. "Santa and all his associates will soon fill those spaces."

"I don't imagine the city charges them rent." She tried to sound light.

"Maybe they could pay in cookies and toys," the mayor teased.

"Pleased to meet you, Ms. Galloway." Mr. Peters politely tipped his head. "I'll see you both at the meeting later."

"What is this morning's meeting about?" Krista asked the mayor as they continued along. She assumed it was to introduce her but wanted to be sure.

"Christmasville, of course. It's right around the corner."

"Oh? I'm surprised the city attorney needs to attend a meeting like that." She frowned. "Is it because there are legal issues involved? Concerns of lawsuit?"

"No, no." He laughed. "It's because Byron runs Santa's toy shop. Naturally, he has to be at the meeting."

Krista had to bite her tongue. Was the mayor actually suggesting that the city paid their attorney to run Santa's toy shop? What on earth was going on here? It looked like everyone in this town was obsessed with Christmasville. Still, she knew it was premature to question them on this. Observation first, determination later. A good city manager knows when to keep quiet and when to speak. A good city manager is diplomatic, optimistic, and a good team player. Her job was not to take over, but to help others to succeed. She could do this. She could.

4

The mayor was just winding up Krista's two-bit tour and about to take her to her new office when he suddenly appeared nervous. "Uh-oh," he muttered under his breath. "I guess it's too late now."

"Too late for what?" she quietly asked.

"To avoid something unpleasant." He lowered his voice. "That, uh, that's Winston Palmer down the hall."

She studied the slight man in the gray suit, walking toward them. He appeared harmless enough.

"He was the other applicant for the city manager position," the mayor whispered.

"Oh." As Winston Palmer got closer, she could see he was older. Perhaps in his fifties, or perhaps just prematurely bald. And he wasn't much taller than her.

Mayor Richards smiled as he greeted him, politely introducing them. "And Winston is the city's chief financial officer."

Winston's lips curved slightly, but his eyes looked chilly as he limply shook her hand. "Pleased to meet you, Ms. Galloway."

"And you too. How long have you worked for the city?" she asked pleasantly.

"Twenty-nine years," he answered stiffly.

"That's very impressive." She nodded, her smile fixed.

"Yes, and I've been around long enough to know the ins and outs of our town." His eyes narrowed slightly. "Long enough to know that Winter Hill does not need a city manager."

"Oh?" She felt her brows arch and regretted it.

"It's nothing personal, Ms. Galloway. But it's no secret that I opposed the idea of hiring a city manager. I had even offered to act as manager myself, meanwhile continuing as CFO—*without* a raise." He scowled at the mayor. "But the committee turned me down. I guess they don't care about fiscal savings or keeping the city out of the red."

"Or perhaps they didn't want to impose on your generosity, Mr. Palmer. The chief financial officer has enough responsibilities without adding the pressures of general management to his load. I should think you'd be relieved."

He made a noise that sounded like "harrumph," then mumbled something about the ten o'clock meeting and continued on his way.

"Well said," the mayor quietly told her. "Looks like you really do have what it takes to be city manager." He glanced over his shoulder. "But be forewarned, Ms. Galloway. Winston Palmer will be your biggest adversary here. If I had my way, we'd send him packing. But I'm only the mayor. And Winston's roots in this town are deep."

"Does Mr. Palmer perform his job well?" she asked.

"Apparently he balances the budget. At least he claims to." The mayor rubbed his chin. "Truth be told, I sometimes wonder if anyone is really paying that much attention. When I get my copy of the yearly budget, I attempt to decipher it, but the fact is I can hardly make heads or tails of all those pages of columns and figures. Frankly it puts me to sleep faster than a hot toddy on a cold winter night."

She chuckled as she pulled out her phone, opening the notepad. "Well, that's just one more reason for a city manager. I'll add this to my to-do list and make it a priority to review last year's budget. Thank you for your insight, Mayor Richards."

"Good for you, Ms. Galloway. I suspect we really do need you here." He peered closely at her. "Do you prefer to be addressed formally? Because I don't mind if you just call me Barry. Or Mayor Barry if you prefer. Or Santa, when the time is right." He chuckled loudly and Krista could almost imagine him dressed up as the jolly old Saint Nick.

She considered his question. So far, the mayor appeared genuine, friendly, and helpful. "I don't mind if you call me Krista," she quietly confessed. "Although I'm not ready for everyone to take such liberties. Not just yet."

"I understand. And I suspect the staffers will mind their manners, attempting to be on their best behavior for our new city manager."

"I do have a question about one staffer." She glanced around to be sure no one could hear her. "About the CFO . . . I'm curious—what sort of role does Mr. Palmer play in Christmasville?"

Mayor Barry's cheery countenance faded. "Between you and me, he'd make an excellent Scrooge. He hates Christmasville."

She repressed the urge to chuckle at the idea of Winston Palmer dressed like Ebenezer Scrooge. And then she realized that she could probably relate to the CFO's disapproval of Christmasville . . . and it did not feel good.

"I'm surprised Winston doesn't go around saying *bah humbug* all the time." The mayor shook his head. "Winston is convinced that Christmasville is a complete waste of time and energy, and worst of all, a waste of city funds. But you'll be hearing all about that before long. Fortunately Winston is a minority. A minority of one."

"Interesting." Hopefully she wouldn't make that two.

"Well, it's nearly ten," Mayor Barry announced as he pointed her toward a pair of double doors. "This is your office. Pauline gave me a sneak peek last week. They fixed it up really nice for you." He pointed down the hall. "And you saw where the conference room is located. So I'll leave you to it."

She thanked him and then, with her Christmasville coffee mug still in hand, went into the office. To her pleasant surprise, it was a corner office with windows looking out over what appeared to be the city park. The pale carpet felt new and the walls and wainscot appeared freshly painted. Her desk was large and attractive, the leather guest chairs looked comfortable, and there was even a console complete with a coffee station and a mini fridge stocked with water, soda, and juice. But the fly in the ointment was the décor. Nine large colorful posters of the previous Christmasville celebrations adorned most of the wall space. Oh, they were handsomely matted and framed, but she assumed they were expected to hang there year-round. Would she ever be able to escape Christmasville?

She refilled her green-and-red coffee mug. Then, with a notepad and pen in hand, she proceeded to the conference room. She hoped they didn't expect her to chair today's meeting, but she braced herself for this possibility. She would simply lead by asking questions and gleaning information. Hopefully they had another plan.

As everyone got settled in the conference room, which not surprisingly was decorated with yet more Christmasville memorabilia, Krista was grateful that Mayor Barry appeared to be chairing this meeting. She knew different cities handled responsibilities and leadership in various ways, and she also knew that Mayor Barry's position was unpaid, but as he called the room to order, he was clearly the respected leader here.

First on his agenda was to introduce the new city manager. And either he'd carefully listened to her earlier or he'd done some independent research, because it was a decent introduction. So much so that she felt no need to mention any of her professional accomplishments or add to his summary. Instead, she simply thanked them for hiring her and told them how impressed she was with Winter Hill.

"I haven't even been here twenty-four hours and I can see this is a delightful place to live. I look forward to serving Winter Hill, and I'm eager to begin learning as much as I can about this wonderful town. I invite all of you to communicate with me any hopes, expectations, suggestions, or concerns that I can help with. I plan to maintain an open-door policy. My primary goal is to assist the city to function as efficiently and positively as possible." She smiled at the mayor. "And now I hand the meeting back to you."

Relieved to sit down and observe, Krista listened as the mayor handed the meeting over to the Christmasville chairwoman. Krista had met Martha Morgan during her two-bit tour. Her first impression was that Martha was a congenial middle-aged children's librarian, but as Martha took over the meeting it became clear that she was energetic, enthusiastic, and a huge fan of Christmasville.

"Before we get to this year's information packet"—she held up the bright red-and-green striped folder—"I'd like everyone on the Christmasville Committee to briefly introduce themselves to Ms. Galloway."

Krista took notes as they went around the crowded table. Although she'd met some of the city staffers present, most of the people represented other venues, including the Chamber of Commerce, various philanthropic groups, and the fire and police departments. Even Beth Seymour, last night's reporter from the newspaper, was there.

Krista thanked them. "It'll be a pleasure getting to know all of you."

Now Martha opened her own folder. "You have before you this year's information packet," she began. "The first few pages include festival positions and responsibilities and a schedule for all our volunteers, including phone numbers and emails so that you can be in communication with each other as needed. As you can see, not all positions are filled. Please, feel free to enlist your friends, family, and neighbors to join the cause. The more the merrier." She flipped through the other sections, explaining their purposes until she came to the last page. "Now, as you all know, we'll be using the first floor of City Hall for some new Christmasville stations. There's a map of the lower level in the back of your notes. The spaces are numbered and will be assigned on a first-come-first-served basis."

Krista listened with amusement as Martha went through the various details—everything from what kind of baked goods would be available in Mrs. Claus's kitchen to the hours the skating rink would be open—but she marveled at how seriously they were taking this planning meeting about elves and reindeer and Santa stand-ins, offering comments, questions, and suggestions appropriately. Clearly everyone in here was on board with this. Well, almost everyone. Across the room from her, Winston Palmer had a disgruntled expression, barely glancing at Martha's information packet and, unless Krista was mistaken, he was getting ready to rain on their Christmas parade.

"Are there any more questions?" Martha asked with a bright smile.

A few more queries were tossed and fielded, but finally there was a tiny lapse and Winston spoke up. "I'd like to see this year's budget for Christmasville. Have you prepared that yet, Martha?"

"Well, not as yet, Winston, but I assume it will be similar to last year's. Although we have some additional costs in regard to—"

"Similar to last year's?" He held up the page with the map of the first floor, waving it back and forth. "How did you plan to cover *this* expense? These offices should've been leased or rented by now. They need to be earning real income—yet you people plan to turn the whole thing into a ridiculous Santa land. Have you ever paused to consider the lost revenue here? And what about the utilities involved? There's heat, water, electrical costs. And that's not all. What about legal liabilities?" He pointed to Byron Peters. "Have you ever considered what it could cost the city if a kid got hurt? And there are dozens of ways that could happen. The ice rink for starters. Or the giant Christmas tree could fall. Kids could be trampled by the live reindeer. Or get food poisoning from some of those homemade foods. The list is endless. A big fat lawsuit could send our city into bankruptcy."

"We have insurance," Byron calmly answered. "And we do have permission forms for some activities. I think we're covering our bases here, Winston."

But Winston was not convinced. He continued to go on what sounded like a well-rehearsed tirade against the waste of Christmasville in general. "Too much money, too much city employee time, too much risk. It's time to put a stop to this nonsense before it puts a stop to Winter Hill." He blustered for a couple more minutes, but finally paused long enough for Mayor Barry to jump in.

"But you're missing something important in your dismal financial forecast, Winston. You fail to recognize what an excellent public relations platform we have created in Christmasville. As we all know, our town was financially floundering after the last recession. The local economy was in the toilet. And we went out on a limb to put together our first Christmasville celebration. Admittedly, we probably went in the hole that year. But the next year was better. And from what I understand, thanks to our volunteers, we've been pretty much breaking even. And thanks to the visitors who've come from as far away as Florida—deciding that Winter Hill is a wonderful place to live—our town's population has steadily increased in the past six years. We all know this is a direct result of Christmasville. It's why we've experienced a recent housing need and subsequent building boom."

"There are some people who feel the town is growing too quickly," Winston argued. "And we have to address the expense of infrastructure improvements and—"

"More homes equals more tax revenue," the mayor shot back. "A stronger economy will make for a stronger tax base. In the end it will equal out—and then some. You can't get bigger without some growing pains. And most people in Winter Hill will agree that our town has only gotten better these last ten years—much of that is thanks to Christmasville."

"You're not running for mayor," Winston said sharply. "Save your campaign speech for the next election."

Suddenly the two men, as well as many others, were arguing so loudly that Krista did the only thing she could think of to put the brakes on. She picked up her nearly empty coffee mug and, using it like a gavel, banged it so soundly onto the conference table that it cracked in several pieces.

"Excuse me!" Suppressing embarrassment over the splashed coffee around the broken Christmas mug, Krista continued. "May I call this meeting to order?"

Everyone grew quiet, looking expectantly her way.

"I have a suggestion." She calmly pointed to Winston. "Why don't you create a spreadsheet that shows the committee exactly what the expenses of Christmasville actually are, as well as a spreadsheet to show the increased tax revenue and other fiscal benefits that the mayor just described. That way we can all see, in black and white, what we are talking about."

Winston scowled at her. "That would take a lot of hours to prepare."

"Are you saying you're too busy to perform this task?" Krista persisted. "Because I'm sure there must be someone in your department that you could delegate to or perhaps we could hire an outside firm to—"

"No, that's not what I meant."

"Then are you saying it's too difficult to pull these figures together?" She tipped her head to one side. "Don't you have access to all these numbers, Mr. Palmer?"

He glared at her. "Even if I do produce these spreadsheets, it's pointless. I tell these people all the time that this silly event is getting far too expensive—but do they listen to me? It's like spitting in the wind."

"Have they ever seen the Christmasville budget numbers on paper?" she demanded. "In an easy-to-read spreadsheet?" She smiled placatingly. "Even if no one else cares to read it, I'm interested."

"I'm interested too," the mayor chimed in. "And I like that *easy-to-read* part. Too bad all our financial reports aren't easy to read."

"I'd like to see it too," Martha said. "But don't forget that a lot of our expenses are covered by donations. Not only in materials and labor, but some folks make cash donations too. Don't forget to include those in your spreadsheet, Winston. And don't forget to include the profits that go back into the general Christmasville fund when it's over and done. I was under the impression that we broke even these last couple of years. Or nearly even."

"That doesn't include using city property like you plan to do this year," he shot back at her. "How do you account for that expense?"

"We need that extra space," a woman from public relations declared. "We're predicting even bigger crowds. We've had nationwide coverage this year. We're even featured in the November issue of *Sunset*." She waved the magazine for emphasis. "That's no small potatoes."

"And we've got that figure-skaters club from Seattle performing on the two weekends before Christmas," someone else pointed out. "That's a ticketed event."

"And so is the concert on the twenty-first," Martha said. "Don't forget that on your spreadsheet."

"So this should be a record-breaking year for Christmasville in Winter Hill," the mayor declared with a big smile. "Thanks to everyone's contributions. There's no reason Christmasville can't be the biggest winter celebration in the Pacific Northwest."

"Unless we get no snow." Winston stood, collecting his things. "You all seem to forget that the success of this winter celebration is directly related to the weather. And, according to the Farmer's Almanac, the northwest is supposed to have a dry winter." He made a smug smile that really would've befitted Ebenezer Scrooge then, excusing himself, exited the room.

"Bah humbug!" Mayor Barry declared after the door was closed.

"What a buzzkill." A young clerk rolled her eyes.

"I don't know why we allow him to attend these meetings," Martha said.

"Let's not let Winston dampen our spirits," the mayor said. "We all know he hates Christmasville." He turned to Krista. "That's a great idea you had about having him make a spreadsheet. For one thing it will keep him busy—gives him less time to grumble at everyone. Besides that, it would be interesting to see the real numbers in an easy-to-read document. Good work, Ms. Galloway." He grinned. "Welcome to the Christmasville team."

She smiled but kept her true thoughts to herself. Sure, it was true that Winston Palmer had some very Scrooge-like qualities. But, to be fair, stinginess wasn't such a bad quality in the person holding the city purse strings. She could imagine how a big celebration like Christmasville could get out of hand. It was always easier for a city to spend than to save—especially when it was an emotional expense. People outside of the finance department tended to think with their hearts, not their heads. But perhaps Krista could help them to understand. She hoped so.

· 5 ·

By the end of her first day, Krista had reached numerous conclusions. The mayor appeared to be friendly and dependable. Her assistant, Pauline Harris, was a valuable advocate. Martha Morgan was enthusiastic, but perhaps not realistic. This was driven home when Martha showed up in Krista's office, with the suggestion that Krista should work in Santa's workshop.

"You're so petite and cute, Ms. Galloway, you'd make a lovely little elf. You could be the head elf during your shifts. And your little daughter could help too. I'm sure she'd love it. Perhaps she could invite some little friends to help too. It would be such fun."

Krista wanted to argue about "fun" but remembered her resolve not to rock anyone's boat during her first week on the job. Instead, she smiled politely and promised to think about it. But at the end of the day as she walked through the dusky town, carrying her recyclable bag filled with milk, eggs, produce, and other heavy grocery items, she felt her mind was made up. Somehow, without offending Martha or being labeled the second-string Scrooge—since Winston had earned that title—she would bow out of volunteering for Christmasville. She would claim she was too busy, or had other plans, or anything to avoid getting pulled into a celebration that opposed everything she believed. Perhaps she could tell them she was ethnically Jewish. Except that wasn't exactly true and she had no intention of lying. To be fair, it could be true. She didn't actually know anything about her birth parents' heritage. She'd been tempted to do a DNA test last year but then heard a story about an adopted adult whose DNA test revealed a birth father who was a serial killer. So Krista nixed that idea. Some stones were better left unturned.

As Krista reached the grade school, she checked her watch. She'd skipped her lunch break and left work a little early in order to grab some groceries and pick up Emily. It wasn't even five o'clock and it was already dark out. She'd known that the sun set earlier in the Northwest, but it would still be daylight in Phoenix right now. And warm. Krista shivered as she hurried up the front steps. Perhaps she'd need to get a car sooner than she'd imagined.

Inside, the school was light and bright and warm. She turned right past the office, like Mrs. Richards had told her, heading for the gymnasium where the after-school program was housed. Expecting to hear children's shrill happy voices, she was surprised—and unsettled—by how quiet it was when she approached the open door. She anxiously peered into the gym, spotting Emily sitting on the floor with a young woman.

"Hello," Krista called out in relief. "I'm here."

"You're here!" Emily exclaimed and, rushing toward her, enveloped her in a hug. "I thought you'd never come."

Krista smiled at the woman. "I hope I'm not late. Mrs. Richards said child care was provided until six."

"That's right." The woman nodded. "But most kids get picked up earlier. I'm Shara, by the way."

Krista introduced herself while helping Emily into her parka. "I actually don't get off work until five. I quit a little early today. But even if I come straightaway, it'll probably be about five fifteen . . . at best."

Shara frowned slightly as she reached for her own coat. "That's okay." Although her tone suggested it was not okay, and it was obvious she wanted to go home too.

Krista quickly thanked her and, picking up Emily's backpack, hurried them from the gym and outside.

"It's nighttime!" Emily exclaimed. "You really were late, Mama."

"It's not actually as late as you think." She explained how it got dark earlier in Washington.

"And it's cold too. Do you think it'll snow?"

"I don't think so. The sky is completely clear." Krista hastened her pace. "If we walk faster, we'll stay warmer."

By the time they reached the apartment, they were both shivering. "I'm going to get us a car," Krista said as she locked the door. Although the apartment was warmer than outside, it was still on the chilly side. Krista turned up the thermostat again. "Ceiling heat," she complained as she unloaded groceries, "is for the birds!"

"What's ceiling heat?"

Krista explained their heating dilemma as she started dinner. "So you wind up with a hot head and cold feet." She handed Emily a slice of cheese. "Dinner will be ready in about twenty minutes. Why don't you go put your coat and pack away and wash your hands. Then you can help me in here and tell me about your day."

By the time they sat down to a simple dinner, Krista felt encouraged. Emily loved her school and her teacher and even felt hopeful about the prospects of friends.

"All the kids were nice, but Laurel is the nicest girl in the whole wide world." Emily forked into her spaghetti. "She showed me where the bathroom was and sat with me at lunch and played with me at recess. I think she's going to be my BFF."

"I hope so." Krista didn't want to tell Emily that Laurel had been assigned to her as an elf buddy, but she also hated to see Emily get her hopes up and then be disappointed.

"And guess what, Mama?" Emily had a spaghetti noodle hanging down her chin.

"What? But don't talk with your mouth full." Krista waited.

Emily chewed and swallowed. "Laurel lives right next to the Christmas House." Her eyes grew wide. "She watched it getting moved last night too. And that house isn't very far from here. So maybe I can go to Laurel's house sometime. Like maybe after school. That would be lots better than the after-school program." Emily frowned.

"You don't like the after-school program?"

"It's okay. But the kids there weren't as nice as the kids in my class. Some of them were mean. And Shara yells too much."

"Oh." Krista felt disappointed. "Well, it was your first day, honey. Maybe it'll be better tomorrow."

"Yeah, but if Laurel asks me to go to her house after school . . . *sometime* . . . can I go?" The twinkle in Emily's eyes was a tip-off.

"Only if Laurel *asks* you, Emily. You cannot ask her. That would be bad manners. And not a good way to start things up with a potential BFF."

"Oh." Emily looked dismayed. "But if *she* asks me, can I go?"

"*May* I go," Krista corrected.

"May I go?" Emily looked up with hopeful blue eyes.

"Only if Laurel's mother has agreed. And then you'll have to call me and get permission, and then I'll have to call Laurel's mother and talk to her."

"Okay." She picked up a piece of broccoli. "I'll do all that. I promise." She nodded. "Now, Mama, how was your day?"

Krista couldn't help but smile at this switch in conversation. Emily was only eight, but she was quite grown up in some ways. So Krista told her a bit about City Hall. And about the Christmasville planning meeting.

"Does that mean you'll be helping with Christmasville?" Emily's eyes lit up.

"Well, I suppose I'll have to . . . a little." Krista had no intention of telling Emily about Martha's suggestion they be elves in Santa's workshop. "As little as possible."

"I know you don't like Christmas." Emily looked uneasy. "But I don't really know why."

Krista felt both defensive and concerned. "What makes you think I don't like Christmas? We always have a tree and presents and everything." Just last night Krista had stuck the box that contained their artificial tree in the laundry room.

"I know, but I can tell you don't really like Christmas. And I just wonder why sometimes."

Krista picked up her empty plate. She wasn't ready for this. Not tonight.

"Is it because your birthday is at Christmastime?"

Krista rinsed her plate, trying to think of a good answer, something Emily could understand. "Well, I've never been that into my birthday, Emily. You know that."

"I know, but I don't get it." Emily brought her plate to the sink. "I love when my birthday comes. I can't wait until May sixth. But when your birthday comes, you don't even tell anyone."

Krista took her plate. "Just because it doesn't really matter."

"But why?" Emily had that stubborn tone in her voice. "I want to know, Mama."

Krista set down the plate and sighed. "It's a long story, honey, and there's—"

"I like long stories." Emily grabbed her hand. "Come sit on the couch and tell me your story."

Krista just shook her head. "Okay, but I'll tell you the short version. I want to get some of those boxes unpacked and put away."

"I'll help you—if you tell me your story *first*."

They made room on the couch and Krista attempted to tell Emily a sanitized version of her unhappy childhood. "Well, you know I didn't have real parents when I was a kid," she began slowly.

"Because you were in foster homes," Emily added.

"That's right." She didn't want to explain that she couldn't be adopted because her parents had never gone through the proper steps . . . because she'd simply been abandoned with no paperwork. "Some of the foster homes weren't too bad. But some had too many kids. And some had other problems. And sometimes I'd finally feel at home and then something would happen . . . and I'd get moved."

"But why did that make you not like Christmas? Or your birthday?"

"Well, I guess because both my birthday and Christmas came at the same time and, well, I was a little kid and I'd get my hopes up really high. I'd think that Santa Claus was coming or something else very special was going to happen. I'd make a wish or dream a dream . . . and then I'd get disappointed." Krista felt a lump in her throat. "So I finally just quit hoping altogether. And I made up my mind that I hated Christmas—and my birthday. I even hated the month of December. Because it always just made me sad. Sadder than anything else. But when January came along, I felt happier." She smiled down on Emily, smoothing her blonde hair away from her face. "But then I started to like Christmas again because of you, Emily." At least she'd tried to like it. She'd pretended to like it. Apparently not well enough. "And I like Christmas because it's supposed to be a day when we remember that God sent us his Son."

"And that should make you happy—that you and Jesus have almost the same birthday."

Krista simply nodded. She didn't think Emily needed to hear that Jesus' real birthday was probably a couple months earlier. And now she needed a way to wrap this up—in a positive way if possible.

"Did it make you even sadder about Christmas, I mean because Daddy left us at Christmastime? And now he's never coming back anymore?"

Krista sighed deeply. She didn't realize that Emily actually remembered it had been shortly before Christmas when Garth had let them down. "Yeah, I suppose that didn't help much, Em. But I'm okay about that. And Daddy has a new life now. Remember I told you he has a new wife." Krista tried hard to conceal her feelings about Emily's father. Even when he failed to pay child support or send his daughter birthday or Christmas gifts, Krista kept quiet about it. She didn't want to turn Emily against her father.

"And you still have me." Emily looked up with wide eyes.

"Thank God, I still have you." Krista hugged her. "And I'll try to be better about Christmas. But it's not easy for me. And you know what they say, honey."

"What?" She tipped her head to the side. "What do they say?"

"You can't teach an old dog new tricks." Krista winked at her.

Emily frowned. "But you're not an old dog, Mama."

"Maybe not, but I'm as tired as an old dog." She reached for a pile of towels. "And you promised you'd help me. Can you go put these in the linen closet by the bathroom?" Relieved to move on, Krista distracted Emily with the setting up of housekeeping. But by the time she tucked Emily into bed, Krista knew that she had to do something to get through her usual seasonal slump. December was right around the corner. And Winter Hill was not a place to shirk from Christmas.

6

The next morning, Beth met Krista at City Hall to get some more photos and finish up her interview. "I wanted to tell you that I thought you did a good job managing the Christmasville planning meeting." Beth chuckled. "I was already creating a front-page story in my head about the mayor and the city's CFO getting into fisticuffs."

"Fisticuffs." Krista laughed. "Now that's not a word you hear every day."

"Well, I am a journalist," Beth teased. "I'm supposed to use big, expensive words."

"Did you get enough about me?" Krista asked. "Not that I didn't enjoy it. But I do have work to do."

"You mean Christmasville work?" Beth asked. "From what I hear that's about all you're expected to be doing for the next few weeks."

"I'm beginning to realize that." She pointed to her ever-growing to-do list. The top priorities this week were regarding the first floor of City Hall. She wanted to make sure that it was safe and operable for Christmasville occupation. She planned to meet with maintenance, the power company, the city attorney, and a few others.

Beth stood. "Well, I've enjoyed getting to know you, Krista. If you ever need a girlfriend to talk to—I mean off the record—let me know."

Krista smiled. "Thank you. I really appreciate that. Maybe we should do lunch sometime."

"Yes, well, there are people who say 'we should do lunch,' and people who actually make it happen. Why don't we set it up now?"

"Okay. Let's do it." Krista pulled up her calendar and they both agreed to lunch at Dasher's Deli on Friday. As Beth left, Krista felt that perhaps this was the beginning of a genuine friendship. Not that Krista had much experience with such things. And the truth was, the idea of it, though intriguing, made her a little nervous.

Krista spent the rest of the day trying to nail down people regarding the use of the offices on the first floor. Finally, she stopped by the city attorney's office. "I know I don't have an appointment with you until tomorrow," she told Byron. "But I just have a quick question."

"Come in," he said pleasantly. "I'm not that busy."

So she went over her worry list with him, explaining concerns she had over using the offices. "The maintenance guys seemed to think I was obsessing," she confessed. "They act like there's no problem. Telling me that the police department was perfectly comfortable here for decades. And maybe that's just the small-town way, to brush things under the rug. But I'm from a big city. And I know this building is old enough to contain asbestos and lead-based paint. The second and third floors have been completely done over, so I assume they're safe. But this first level, well, it doesn't appear to have been touched in years. I doubt the police force gave it much thought."

"Interesting." Byron glanced around his office. "I never actually considered those possibilities myself. I suppose I should look into having this place checked."

"I don't want to scare you." She pointed to the ceiling. "But those tiles could have asbestos. And the flooring might as well."

Byron frowned. "So what do you want me to do?"

"Well, the maintenance crew seems to be dragging their heels. Naturally, they're used to going through the standard protocol of paperwork, requests, financial analysis—you know, the slow-moving wheels of city progress. You're using a space down here. And you're obviously concerned about your own health." She pointed to a framed photo of an attractive woman and toddler on his desk. "At least I'll assume that they are."

"That's true." He nodded. "So you want me to do some checking here, in my own office?"

"Would you?"

He rubbed his chin. "I'd be afraid not to now." He stood up. "In fact, I think I'll take an early lunch and find someone to look into it immediately. I'd been meaning to do some improvements in here. In fact, my wife already picked out paint samples and has offered to do it. She loves to paint. But if it's dangerous, I don't want her in here either."

"Or that pretty little girl."

He was already loading his briefcase. "I don't know whether to thank you or get mad," he said as he reached for his coat.

"Well, hopefully we'll find out that it's perfectly safe." She followed him out. "And as the city attorney, I'm sure you'd be relieved to know we're not endangering children and families who come traipsing through here for Christmasville. Otherwise we might as well wait for Halloween and call this the House of Horrors."

He groaned. "Oh, that's awful."

"Thank you for checking it out," she told him. "And please keep this between you and me. No point in frightening anyone until we know for sure. Hopefully we can figure it out quickly. Christmasville is due to open in less than two weeks."

"Well, we've always had it outside in the past." They walked toward the front entrance together. "But last year we had such a blizzard during the second week that the kiosk that housed Mrs. Claus's kitchen collapsed. And a couple of the tented booths nearly blew away in the high winds. Of course, everyone made the best of it and the excess snow was great for the snow-sculpting contest. But it was a relief to think we could house so much of the festivities indoors this year." He sighed. "My little Janie is really looking forward to Christmasville. She's almost four. But naturally, I'd want her to be safe."

"Naturally," she said.

Before he exited, he promised to get back to her as soon as he got a report. She thanked him then headed for the elevator. She'd immediately found the first floor of City Hall a bit unsettling yesterday, but had kept her thoughts to herself. At first she thought it simply had to do with its history. A police station probably had some hard stories . . . if walls could talk. And she knew that one section had originally been used for jail cells, although those were gone now. Still, if it was dangerous as far as toxicity, the city would be foolish to use it for Christmasville. Even if no real harm came from it, anyone could press a lawsuit if they wanted. Especially if they learned of the inherent and neglected dangers. At least Byron could respect that.

By Wednesday afternoon, Krista had made up her mind. "I've got to find a car," she told Pauline during their coffee break.

"You don't have a car?" Pauline looked shocked. "I had no idea."

"Well, I hate to complain. And I thought Emily and I could get by for a while. But it's just too hard. I didn't realize how early it gets dark here. And then there's the cold."

"Of course, you need a car." Pauline set down her coffee. "My brother over in Spokane has a big lot. Both new and used cars. I'll bet he could find you a good deal. Do you know what you're looking for?"

"Something small, I suppose. With good fuel economy. And good in this climate."

"Why don't I give him a call for you?" Pauline pulled out her phone. "Then, if you like, I could drive you over to look around."

"You wouldn't mind?"

"Not at all. I'd love to see Rodney."

After work, Pauline drove Krista and Emily to Spokane to see the cars that Rodney had handpicked for Krista to look at. He led them around the lot, explaining the differences between models, finally stopping by a bright red car.

"Ooh," Emily cooed. "This is beautiful."

"I don't know." Krista frowned. She did not want a bright red car.

"But it's so pretty. It looks like a Christmas car."

Krista grimaced. She definitely did not want a Christmas car.

"This is a Prius," Rodney told her. "And based on what Pauline told me, I thought it might be your best bet, but I only have one on the lot right now. They're pretty popular. If you're interested in this one, I can give you a really good deal on it. It's actually last year's model. This, uh, color wasn't as popular as I'd expected."

Krista could understand that.

"Please, Mama," Emily begged. "It's so pretty. Lots prettier than the other cars."

"Go ahead and try it out." He opened the doors, waiting for them to get inside.

"Oh, Mama, it's so nice." Emily ran her hands over the dashboard and console. "And it smells so clean and new. Can't we get it? *Please?*"

"I have heard good things about these cars," Krista admitted.

"The man said he'll give us a good deal."

Krista really was determined to leave this place with a car—but a bright red one?

"I prayed for God to give us a car for Christmas," Emily told her with solemn sincerity. "Don't you think this is the one? It looks like a Christmas car to me."

Krista couldn't help but laugh. "Well, I can't argue with that. It's a very Christmassy color."

"See. Then we should get it."

After a test drive and hearing more of Rodney's reasoning,

Krista gave in. And after going through the paperwork, with a dinner of hot dogs and stale potato chips, she and Emily were driving back to Winter Hill in a bright red *Christmas car*. Emily could not have been happier. Krista was somewhat dumbfounded.

On Thursday morning, Krista could tell by Byron's face that the news was not good. "Just get it over with," she said after he sat down. "Like tearing off a bandage."

"There's asbestos in the floor and ceilings. Not everywhere. Some of the spaces had been updated over the years. But the old ceiling tiles and a lot of the flooring contain asbestos. And a few of the walls have lead paint."

"Oh, dear." She drummed her fingers on her desk, trying to think.

"It's a good thing you asked about this." Byron sighed.

"So now what? Not that this is your problem."

"Actually it is. My office needs abatement too."

"Right. And that raises another question, Byron. What about the city's culpability for when the police force occupied the space? I know asbestos is carcinogenic. And lead is toxic. Does the city bear any liability since the city owns the building? And the police are city employees."

"It's a good question. I wondered about that myself. I'm already looking into the legalities."

"Thank you." She shook her head. "But what about Christmasville? We can't very well open that space to the public now."

"That's for sure."

"But it's not really your problem." She reached for her phone.

"Although I would appreciate a report from you regarding our liability concerns."

"I'll get you a report as soon as I can. Give me a couple of weeks." He frowned. "In the meantime, I think we should keep a lid on this."

"How is that done?" she asked him. "The whole Christmasville Committee will want to know why we can't use the space." She sighed. "I feel like I've opened a real can of worms."

"Well, it's your can of worms." His smile looked sympathetic. "Welcome to Winter Hill." He set a business card on her desk. "This is the abatement company that did the inspection. The contractor is a friend of mine and he'll send you the report. His name is Owen Payne. And he's offered to prepare a bid."

"Thanks." She picked up the card, quickly constructing a plan. "I'll call together an emergency meeting as soon as possible. Maybe this afternoon. I hope you can come."

"You bet." He opened the door. "Good luck."

As soon as he left, Krista asked Pauline into her office, sharing the bad news. "I want a meeting with all department heads—including maintenance—as well as the mayor. Tell them it's an emergency meeting. This afternoon, if possible."

"Will do." Pauline nodded.

"In the meantime, I'll have a chat with the abatement contractor."

By two o'clock, Krista was presenting the problem to the department heads. She brought them up-to-date and shared copies of Owen Payne's report. "And he's promised to get me a bid for the work ASAP. He and his guys are down there right now."

"That was quick," Mayor Barry said with a worried expression.

"Well, they were already on it so it seemed a good idea."

"You're only getting one bid?" Winston questioned her.

"One for today. Certainly we'll have others." She nodded to Pauline, who was taking meeting notes. "You already contacted two other companies, right?"

"That's right."

"The immediate concern is that it probably puts the kibosh on Christmasville down there," Krista said.

"But what if we get it all fixed by then?" the mayor asked.

"The opening of the festival is just over a week away. I don't see how it can possibly be fixed by then."

"Why not?" he persisted. "What if we got several teams working, all at once? I'll bet they could get it cleared out in a day or two. Then the maintenance crew could get in there and put it back together in no time."

"That doesn't sound realistic to me." She turned to Jack Leland, the head of maintenance. "What do you think?"

He slowly shook his head. "Doesn't sound realistic to me either."

"And what about the budget?" Winston asked. "I strongly recommend we delay any abatement until the end of this fiscal period. Wait until March or even later."

"But you were the one concerned over the office spaces sitting vacant," Krista reminded him. "Why would you want to delay it longer than necessary?"

"Because it's prudent."

"What about Christmasville?" the mayor demanded. "Are we going to let everyone down? Our volunteers planned to start working on the spaces in the upcoming weekend and throughout next week. What do we tell them?"

"Tell them there's been a change in plans." Krista pointed to Byron. "Would you please give your legal opinion on this?"

Byron explained his concerns and findings, finally reminding everyone that for the time being, the information was to be kept confidential.

"This is bad, bad, bad." The mayor shook his head. He frowned at Krista. "Couldn't you have waited to discover this until *after* Christmas?"

"You'd let innocent children into those dangerous spaces?" she asked. "Just to celebrate Christmasville?"

"Well, no, of course not. It's just that it's so disappointing."

"I understand." She tried to appear more concerned than she felt. It wasn't that she wanted to shut down Christmasville completely, but she still had concerns about how this event appeared to dominate the town. It showed up everywhere she looked. Was that healthy? She attempted a smile. "Would you mind informing the Christmasville Committee? I think it would be easier to hear coming from you."

"Isn't that a bit like Santa Claus canceling Christmas?" he said.

"It's not as if all of Christmasville is canceled," she reminded him. "Just the part that was going to take place downstairs."

"I think we should cancel the whole thing," Winston declared. "Think of the revenue the city would save."

Mayor Barry glared at Winston, looking as if he wanted to take him to task, but to Krista's relief, he kept his thoughts to himself.

"Well, unless anyone has any other questions or suggestions, let's adjourn this meeting. Pauline will get a copy of the abatement bid to you as soon as we have it." She stood, taking in the glum faces around the table. Well, except for

Winston, who wore a smug look. "I'm sorry to be the bearer of bad news," she said. "But it is what it is." She quickly gathered her paperwork and exited the room. Her fourth day on the job and she was already the bad guy. Winston might be Scrooge, but she was the Grinch . . . stealing Christmas.

7

Instead of returning to her office, Krista went downstairs to speak to Owen Payne. Something had occurred to her at the end of that unpleasant meeting. But she didn't want to tell the others her idea yet, especially since she didn't know whether it was even viable.

"We're nearly done with our measurements," Owen told her as they stood outside of the elevator. "I'll crunch the numbers as soon as we're done, and hopefully have something for you. Perhaps by tomorrow. I know this is a rush job."

She thanked him then waved her hand to the foyer around them. "What about this space?" she asked. "Any asbestos or lead in here?"

"Thankfully, no. And the elevator is clean too."

"That's a relief. So staffers and visitors to the library and city are safe to pass through here?"

"Probably. But it would be a good idea to have asbestos-free areas thoroughly cleaned by my team. Just in case any particles have gone airborne from an affected area. The hallways and front bathrooms are asbestos and lead free too. And the break room and kitchen are okay, as well as the offices that were remodeled. Again, I think they'll all need a thorough cleaning, but that can happen when the abatement is complete."

"So, on your report, can you specifically list the spaces in need of abatement and the spaces that are clean and safe?"

"Sure. That's not a problem."

"Because I'm wondering . . . what if there were a way to temporarily contain the contaminated spaces and still be able to utilize the others—the ones that are clean? That way we could still host Christmasville in here—and do the abatement afterward. Do you think that's feasible? Or am I crazy?"

"That's an interesting idea, but I'm not sure it's possible." He rubbed his chin. "Let me do some research and get back to you. Between the state and the feds, there are a lot of regulations for abatement procedures. I don't want to give you false hopes."

"Well, if you discover it's doable, can you give me a separate bid for that?" she asked. "Like stage one and stage two?"

"Sure." He made a note of this. "I'll try to have it ready by the end of the day tomorrow."

"And, again, I want to remind you of our confidentiality agreement. We don't want the whole town to hear about what's going on down here. Might put a real damper on Christmasville."

"I've already told my team that mum's the word."

She thanked him then headed back up to her office. Although she felt encouraged, she knew it was too soon to celebrate. She did share her news with Pauline though. "As soon as Owen sends that report, I want to see it," she told her.

"The mayor scheduled the Christmasville Committee for an emergency meeting tomorrow morning at ten. He expects you to be there, Krista, to give your report."

"You mean to deliver the bad news." Krista frowned. "So I can be the Grinch."

Pauline patted her on the back. "Like you said, it is what it is. And, one more thing." She glanced to Krista's closed door. "Winston wants to talk to you in private. He asked me to let him know when you got back. Do you want to see him?"

"Do I have a choice?"

Pauline shrugged.

"Go ahead and call him."

Pauline left and within minutes, Winston appeared at her door. She politely invited him in, waiting for him to sit. "What can I do for you?"

"You can recommend to the Christmasville Committee that it's time to put the brakes on their celebration."

"You know that's not going to happen. All the festivities they usually have outside can still take place as planned. It's only the first floor that—"

"That means we'll have to put out funds for new kiosks and all sorts of other expenses. One of the positives about using the first floor was to save money." He scowled. "Although it makes more sense to lease those spaces."

"Except for the asbestos issue."

"Yes, well, that's another problem. But I really do feel that you, as city manager, can exercise the authority to recommend that Christmasville take the year off. It's the prudent thing to do."

"I don't see that as my job," she informed him. "If this were only a city function, maybe . . . but don't forget there are others involved. The Chamber, the newspaper, the philanthropic groups." She held up her hands. "It's a community affair."

"But as city manager, aren't you supposed to advise the city?

Why don't you recommend that it's time the city removes our support of this money-pit celebration? Let the community own it if they want to, but let the city step out. The liabilities alone are reason enough to put the brakes on. What if someone got hurt? And imagine if you hadn't discovered about the asbestos—what kind of lawsuit could occur when folks got wind of that?"

"The truth is I'm not a big fan of Christmasville either," she admitted, hoping that she could win him over by this confession. "I do understand what you're saying. Perhaps it would be wise for the city to step aside and allow the community to own Christmasville. But I haven't even been here a week. I can't very well recommend pulling the plug. Maybe next year."

"I see." Winston looked thoroughly disgruntled now. Had he really expected to convince her to take his side? "Well, perhaps when you see the numbers . . . just how much Christmasville costs us each year. Maybe that will change your mind." He shook a fist. "I'm telling you, Ms. Galloway, it's like pouring water down a rat hole. The city can't afford it year after year. You'll see."

"Great." She forced a smile. "I can't wait to see your financial report. And while we're on the subject, didn't Pauline request a copy of last year's budget?"

"Yes. I'm, uh, working on it." He focused on removing what looked like an imaginary piece of lint from his tie.

"Working on it?" She frowned. "Isn't it just a matter of printing it out? I want *last* year's budget, Winston. Not this year's."

"I'm well aware of that." He looked up with narrowed eyes.

"Or tell me how I can access it on the computer," she said pleasantly. "I haven't seen any financial group docs, but you must have them."

"The City of Winter Hill isn't quite that electronically evolved yet."

"Maybe that should be a goal," she suggested. "It wouldn't just save time, it would save paper. And ultimately it would save money too."

"Right." He sounded seriously irritated.

"Or you could just email me a digital doc. I prefer working on paper, but I can have Pauline print it for—"

"You'll get your hard copy," he snapped. "I'll ask my assistant *again*."

"Thank you." She studied him as he left her office. She couldn't put her finger on it, but something about his demeanor felt somewhat sneaky, or slippery, or untrustworthy. Did Winston have something to hide? Or was she just being overly suspicious?

By noon on Friday, Krista was ready for a break. As she walked to Dasher's Deli to meet Beth for lunch, she replayed her frustrating morning. She'd barely hung up her coat when Winston Palmer stepped into her office, making her wonder if she should rethink her open-door policy. Although Winston still hadn't given her a budget report doc, he did have some new excuses. But the real purpose of his visit was to win her over to his side. Relentless in his opposition to the city's involvement in Christmasville, Winston had created a list of ten reasons why it was time to pull the plug.

Although she actually agreed with some of his logic, she diplomatically told him she'd think about it. But later, when she'd met with the Christmasville Committee, she wondered if Winston wasn't actually on the right track. Naturally, Mayor

Barry—who was acting quite chilly—insisted that Krista be the one to inform the committee that they'd have to find another location for Christmasville. And Martha Morgan, previously the congenial children's librarian, was very upset by the news. She'd grown even more angry when Krista offered no explanation. In fact, the whole committee was upset. They acted as if Krista were personally responsible for their disappointment and changed plans. She couldn't get out of there fast enough.

As much as Krista had wanted to give the committee a smidgeon of hope, she still hadn't heard back from Owen Payne on the possibility of using the clean part of the first floor. And she didn't want to elevate their hopes only to dash them later. Even her own online research had yielded no firm answers. Although some websites described how to temporarily confine an asbestos area, others warned that occupancy in attached areas was dangerous—which made her wonder about the safety of City Hall in general. Perhaps they were all at risk.

"You look perplexed," Beth said as she joined Krista at a table in back. "Hard week?"

"It's had its ups and downs. That's for sure." Krista sighed as she set down her phone. "If you don't mind, I'd rather not talk about work right now. I could use a break."

"Absolutely." Beth smiled as she sat down. "So how is Emily doing? Is she getting settled in?"

Relieved for a distraction, Krista gave Beth the lowdown on her daughter, telling her how much Emily loved her new school and new teacher and new best friend. "The only negative is the after-school care. Emily is not a fan." She shook her head. "I don't know what to do about that. Fortunately, she's been invited to her friend's house for the afternoon today. I just met Laurel Myers' mother yesterday. She seemed very nice."

"Jessie Myers is a good friend of mine. She's a delight. I'm so glad Emily has made friends with Laurel. That's perfect."

"And I'm hoping with a couple days off during the weekend, she'll be ready for the after-school care again by Monday. I honestly don't know what else to do."

"I know what you mean. But there are a couple of options to occupy kids after school. Like dance lessons or karate or art class. And there's the park and rec's swim team—my boys are involved in that. Although Emily's probably a little young. Or you could always look for a babysitter."

"Good ideas. I asked Emily to hang in there until winter break, but that's almost a month away. And then I'll need to find full-time care for her."

"It's such a hassle being a single parent." Beth paused as their orders were set down. "Believe me I know."

"You're single too?"

"Yep. Divorced about six years ago. He's remarried with two step-kids and a new baby on the way. Fortunately, he lives less than a mile away and still likes spending time with his own sons. And my boys get along pretty well with their step-sibs." She shrugged. "So I guess it could be worse. How about your ex? Does he stay involved with Emily?"

"He and his new wife live in Atlanta. He keeps promising to help with child support and to see Emily when he can, but it never seems to happen. Not like he says it will anyway. I try not to get her hopes up."

"Poor Emily. That must be hard on her."

"She's pretty resilient." Krista sighed. "To be honest, I don't really mind that he's out of the picture. In a way, it makes life simpler. Although I'm concerned it could hurt Emily in the long run. If he ever gets to the place where he wants a relationship with his daughter, I won't stand in the way. But for now, it's easier to just be on our own."

They continued to visit as they ate, and before she knew it the lunch hour was over. "That was so nice," she told Beth as they walked outside. "It's great getting to know you."

"Maybe we should make this a regular thing." Beth smiled.

"I'd love to." Krista paused as Beth checked her phone.

"Looks like an interesting story breaking at the high school," Beth told her. "I better go check it out. But let's be sure to do this again, Krista. Real soon, okay?"

Krista agreed and then they parted ways. She wasn't eager to get back to work. It had already been a long week. Not at all what she'd imagined for a small-town city manager. But at least it hadn't been boring. She stopped by Pauline's desk on her way into her office. "Any word back from Owen Payne?" she quietly asked.

"Nothing."

"What about the other contractors?" Krista asked. "Have any agreed to come in and give bids?"

"My son is down there right now." Pauline shuffled through some mail. "I hope you don't mind that I asked him. Conner's pretty busy these days, but he promised to come during his lunch break. He's been down there about an hour. At the very least, he'll give us a bid that can compare to Payne's."

"Yes, the more bids, the better. Thank you."

"And Conner reminded me that next week is Thanksgiving. He wondered if you and Emily had any plans."

"No, I haven't given it a thought."

"Then why don't you join us out on the farm? I'll bet Emily would enjoy playing with our kids."

"You have other kids? Or do you mean grandkids?"

Pauline laughed. "Well, Anna will be there, but she doesn't consider herself a kid anymore. She's our only grandchild, although my daughter Julia has been talking about it lately. But I was referring to baby goats. *Goat* kids."

"You raise goats?"

"My husband does. After he retired from the construction business, he turned into a full-time farmer. And for some reason he has a penchant for goats. I must admit the kids are a lot of fun, but a lot of work too. Still, that's Roy's problem, not mine. Keeps him out of trouble."

"Well, I'm sure Emily would love to see your kids. And we'd love to join you for Thanksgiving. Let me know what we can bring."

"Yes, as soon as I figure it out—" She paused for her phone. "Looks like Winston calling again. You want to take this in your office?"

Krista grimaced. "Or not at all. Tell him I'm out, Pauline. I want to duck down to the first floor to see if Conner can shine any more light on our challenge." She glanced over her shoulder, realizing she'd have to walk past Winston's office in order to use the elevator. She held up her phone. "Call me if you hear back from Owen Payne." And without looking back, she hurried toward the stairwell. Hopefully Winston wouldn't spot her and follow.

8

Krista found Conner emerging from one of the offices with an UNSAFE TO OCCUPY sign on the door. "Don't you need a mask or something in there?" she demanded.

"As long as no one's stirring up dust, it's relatively safe." His brow creased slightly. "So, how are you doing, Krista? All settled in? Everything going okay?"

"Sorry. I guess that wasn't a very friendly greeting. But I've been pretty stressed over the situation down here." She attempted a smile. "And I really do appreciate you taking time to look around."

"Well, I've got all the measurements. It's helpful that Owen Payne marked the rooms in need of abatement. Saves time." He held up his notepad. "I should be able to get an estimate to you by the end of the day."

"Really? That soon?"

"Well, I know it's a big deal—what with Christmasville and all. And it's good you've got Payne on it too. He's dependable. If he's got time to get right on it, you couldn't do any better.

But I understand the need for comparable bids—and to get it abated quickly."

"Yes, absolutely." She nodded. "Do you have time for a few questions?"

"Buy me a cup of coffee and I'm all yours." He checked his watch. "Well, for a while anyway. Got a date with an inspector at two thirty. But we're meeting here in City Hall. After I'm done with that, I'll go over my notes. I should have something for you before five."

"Wonderful." She pointed toward the front door. "I noticed a coffee shop across the street, but I haven't been there yet. Is it any good?"

"Cupid's Coffee. My favorite."

"At first I thought Cupid's had to do with Valentine's Day, but then I started to wonder . . . is it by any chance related to Santa's reindeer?" she asked as they crossed Main Street.

He chuckled. "So you're just figuring this out?"

"Well, I'm starting to put two and two together. I mean there's Dasher's Deli and Comet's Drive-In."

"And there's Blitzen's Bakery, Vixen's Hair Salon, Dancer's Shoe Store, Rudolph's Restaurant, and, let me think . . . oh, yeah, Donner's Dress Shop." He grinned as he opened the door for her. "The Chamber came up with that plan a few years ago. There was some friendly competition over the Rudolph name, but the Chamber head flipped a coin and it all worked out in the end."

They'd barely gotten their coffees and settled into a table by the front window before Krista began to pepper him with questions. He finally held up his hands to stop her. "Okay, let me field those one at a time. For starters, it is feasible to use the spaces that have already been abated. But only if the contaminated spaces are completely sealed off. And that should be fairly easy to do."

"So we could get right on it then? Sealing off the unsafe areas?"

"I don't see any reason why not. If Payne is too busy, I can send a couple of guys over. As soon as tomorrow morning, if that's helpful."

"Really? You'd do that?"

"Absolutely. I'm a big fan of Christmasville. I'd hate to see this put the nix on it. Everyone has really been looking forward to setting up the shops and stations indoors this year. Some people, including my dad, have been working for months on decorations and props and things. This weekend was supposed to be the beginning of setting it all up. It's no wonder the committee was upset."

"I know." She nodded. "And I realize they only had a week to get it all put together. Believe me, I understand their frustration. Martha Morgan pounded that into me this morning." She told him about informing the committee. "The hard thing was not being able to tell them why. They were so mad at me—I'm sure they wanted to tar and feather me and drive me out of town."

He laughed. "That's not a very Christmassy attitude."

She frowned. "What about my concerns for the rest of City Hall?" she reminded him. "The library and city offices?"

"We need to ask the maintenance team about the building's heating system and how the ducts are laid out. That's a legitimate concern, Krista. But even if the ducts are connected, it shouldn't be difficult to seal off the first floor. It might mean no heat down there until after the abatement, but that shouldn't be a problem. Even for Christmasville. People will be dressed warmly since part of the festival is outside anyway."

"And it's supposed to be the North Pole. So it should be cold."

"That's right." He grinned.

"So do you think they can hold Christmasville as planned?"

"I honestly don't see why not. If everything's sealed off. And if the doors are locked so no one can get into them. It should be okay. But while I'm meeting with my inspector this afternoon, I'll run the whole thing past him. He's head of the Building Division so he should know the answers."

Krista was so relieved she felt like hugging him. "I really, really appreciate this, Conner. Anything you can do to get Christmasville back on track is fabulous. The committee and the whole town will be grateful. I didn't want to be the Grinch who stole Christmas."

He chuckled. "No, the new city manager playing Grinch would not sit well with anyone." Krista asked a few more of her questions and mentioned her concerns, but before long it was time for him to get up to the Building Division. They returned to the top floor of City Hall, then shook hands and parted ways.

"How did it go?" Pauline asked Krista.

"Your son is a wonder." Krista unbuttoned her coat. "Any word from Payne yet?"

"Not yet."

"What did Winston want? Did he have that budget report?"

"He wanted to talk to you, but he didn't say a word about the report."

"I'm going to call the mayor now." Krista opened her office door. "I don't want to be disturbed."

"Yes, ma'am." Pauline made a mock salute. "I'll hold 'em at bay."

Krista told Mayor Barry the latest news. "It's probably premature to give the committee the green light yet," she said finally, "but it looks good. Conner's talking to the head of the Building Division right now."

"That's great to hear, Krista. Will you call me as soon as you hear back? I'll notify the committee."

Krista hung up then went to work reading through the city charter and a mountain of other documents that she'd requested Pauline round up for her. She wanted to understand the ins and outs of Winter Hill. The only document missing was the budget.

It was getting close to five when Conner stuck his head into her office. "I've got some answers," he told her.

"Come in." She set down the report she was studying.

"Rod, the head of the Building Division, agrees that we should be able to seal off the areas affected with asbestos or lead. We invited the head of maintenance up to meet with us and it looks like we can shut down the heat on the entire first floor. They'll put some space heaters in the restrooms when the temps drop too low."

"That's great news."

"I just gave Owen Payne a call. He's busy with a big abatement project over at the window factory and he was happy to hand off the first stage of this project to my guys. We're busy too, but I think if I bring my whole team in tomorrow, we can finish it up in a day. The Christmasville volunteers can start setting up as soon as Sunday. Then Owen, or whichever contractor is chosen, can do the full abatement sometime after Christmas." He smiled. "How's that sound?"

"Perfect. Thank you so much."

"Great. I'll let you get back to it then." He frowned at the stacks of paperwork. "Looks like you've got plenty to do."

"Just trying to get up to speed." She thanked him again and

then, as soon as he left, she called Mayor Barry back, sharing the good news. Then she closed up her office and went to pick up Emily. But for some reason, Laurel's mother didn't act very pleased to see her as she let her into the house. "The girls should be down shortly."

"Thanks so much for having Emily." Krista smiled brightly. "I know how much she's been looking forward to it. I hope she was no trouble."

"Emily was fine," Jessie said crisply.

Krista glanced around the large foyer, noticing that it was already decorated for Christmas. "Your home is so beautiful," she said. "I love Victorian architecture."

"Thank you."

Krista studied Jessie's rather grim expression. "Is something wrong?" she asked. "You seem upset."

"Oh, well, I just heard the news."

"News?"

She folded her arms in front of her. "That you've informed the committee we can't use the first floor of City Hall for Christmasville. And you, being new in town, probably don't realize what a blow that is for us."

"Wow, word travels fast. But you haven't—"

"Some of us have been preparing for months and it's just so—"

"Excuse me, Jessie, but you haven't heard the latest news." Krista explained about the plan to make some of the building useable. "It's just that some of the spaces aren't safe for occupancy. And I'm sure that you—or anyone else on the committee—wouldn't want to endanger children."

Jessie blinked. "No, of course not. But no one mentioned that. Everyone just assumed the new city manager was exercising her authority."

Krista pursed her lips.

"But we were obviously wrong." Jessie smiled as the girls came clomping down the stairs. "Forgive me," she said quietly.

"Do I have to go home?" Emily asked Krista.

"Of course you have to go home." Krista smiled stiffly. "But I don't blame you, honey. Laurel's house is very lovely."

Emily pointed to the garland decorating the stair rail. "I wish our apartment looked Christmassy too."

"Yes, I'm sure you do." Krista forced a smile for Jessie. "We're not even completely unpacked yet." She helped Emily into her parka. "But maybe if we get everything put away this weekend, we'll find some Christmas decorations to put up."

Emily brightened. "Can we put our tree up too?"

"It's not even Thanksgiving," Krista reminded her.

"I know, but lots of people have Christmas stuff already."

Krista thanked Jessie as she ushered her daughter out the door. "Well, we'll see," she said as they went outside. "Right now I'm hungry. I thought maybe we'd get some dinner at Comet's Drive-In."

"Yes! Yes!" Emily jumped up and down. "But first I want you to come see the Christmas House."

"Christmas House?"

"You know, the one we watched getting moved." Emily pointed next door.

"Oh, yes, I nearly forgot about that." Krista peered over to the darkened yard. "But I don't see any lights on, and it's too dark to see anything right now."

"Laurel and I got to see it when we came home from school. They already got it painted and it's so pretty. The outside is red and green—like a real Christmas House."

"Red and green?" Krista opened the car door for Emily.

"I'm not sure I'd like that." It actually sounded rather garish. Krista wondered what the neighbors would think.

"And the inside is getting all fixed up too," Emily continued as Krista started the car. "They let me and Laurel walk through the whole house. There's a big fireplace in the living room. It got kind of cracked when they moved it, but an old man was fixing it all up. And the floors are shiny wood. And they were making the kitchen all pretty and new. And Anna's grandpa was there too. He was painting one of the bedrooms. It has three bedrooms, Mama. We've never had three bedrooms before."

Krista chuckled. "We don't need three bedrooms. Two is plenty."

"But if we win the house, you could probably find something to do with another bedroom."

"We're not going to win the house," Krista told her.

"We might win it."

"I honestly don't see how."

"But I've been praying we'll win it."

Krista took in a slow breath. She didn't want to crush her little girl's dreams, but she did want Emily to be realistic. "I don't know much about the contest, honey," she said slowly. "But I suspect that city employees are ineligible."

"Ineligible? What's that mean?"

"That means that I'm probably not allowed to enter the contest." Krista turned into the lot for the drive-in restaurant. "But let's not worry about that now." She distracted Emily by asking what they should order. Then as they waited for their food, Krista told Emily about their Thanksgiving invitation. "Pauline and Roy are Anna's grandparents," she told her. "And Anna will be there too. But the best part is the kids."

"There'll be kids there?" Emily asked hopefully.

Krista explained about the baby goats. "I guess there are a lot of them."

"I've always wanted to pet a real goat," Emily declared. "And baby goats are even better."

Krista felt that, for the moment at least, she'd managed to set her daughter straight. Without too much pain. Emily would discover soon enough that some dreams truly were impossible . . . some hopes just too big. Life inevitably held disappointments. It was inescapable. Hopefully not too much in the near future, but eventually. But for now they had a new red car and a delicious dinner at the drive-in. Not bad for their first week in Winter Hill.

9

After a quiet weekend of getting the apartment in order—and putting up a few Christmassy things—Krista felt ready to return to work. But as she entered the City Hall building, she was surprised to be met by the mayor. And even more surprised to see that the foyer was decorated for Christmas. She was greeted by giant candy canes, draped garlands with big red bows, a family of snowmen, and even a life-sized plywood sleigh.

"The elves have been busy," Mayor Barry told her. "Some started setting things up yesterday."

"It's starting to look a lot like Christmas," she said wryly.

The mayor chuckled. "That reminds me, I want to bring my boom box in from my pickup. I promised to provide Christmas music."

"I'm curious," she said quietly. "Am I still perceived as the Grinch? Should I be watching my back?"

His face grew more serious. "As much as I hate to admit it, Krista, you've made a bad first impression with some folks. But I'm sure you can remedy that easily enough."

"How?"

"For starters, why don't you offer to help out with Christmasville? Martha told me that she'd invited you and your little girl to play elves, but that you turned your nose up at it."

"Turned my nose up?" She frowned. "I told her I'd think about it."

"Same thing—to her." He smiled. "How about it, Krista? It would be a nice goodwill gesture. And I'll bet your little girl would enjoy it."

"Fine," she said a bit stiffly. "Tell Martha that Emily and I will be elves for her. Just have her let me know where and when we're needed, and we'll be there."

"Good for you." He walked her to the elevator. "And I'll try to spread the word that you were instrumental in getting this place useable. Did you remember that tonight is City Council?"

"Oh, that's right." She pressed the up button. "Thanks for the reminder." She knew it was one of the city manager's many responsibilities to attend council meetings, but she'd hoped they might excuse her for this week. Apparently not.

Krista greeted Pauline. "Looks like your son saved the day."

"He and his crew." She frowned. "But not everyone is happy about it."

"Winston?"

"Yes, he already came by, expressing his opinion."

Krista nodded to her office. "Want to give me a quick heads-up?"

Pauline followed her in and quickly explained that Winston complained about the fact that Krista had overstepped her boundaries by hiring Conner's company to begin the abatement. "And you allowed them to do the work without authorization."

"Seriously?" Krista hung up her coat. She'd actually wondered about this, but the situation had looked so dire. Winter Hill was a small town—and Christmasville was such a big thing. She hadn't expected anyone to complain. Well, other than the CFO. "Winston sure seems determined to live up to his Scrooge reputation—and overly eager to shoot down Christmasville."

"And you too, I'm afraid."

"Why am I not surprised?" She sat down on the edge of her desk. "But what can I do about it?"

"I have an idea."

"I'm all ears." Krista waited as Pauline explained how Conner's dad had helped with Saturday's crew.

"Roy was glad to donate his time on Saturday," Pauline continued. "And I don't see why Conner can't donate his company's time too. After all, it's tax deductible. And lots of citizens donate services and materials for Christmasville."

"Oh, that would be wonderful, Pauline. Do you think he'd mind?"

"I can give him a call and find out."

"Thank you so—" She paused at the sound of knocking.

"That's probably Winston," she said quietly. "He said he was coming right back." Pauline opened the door.

"Come in, Winston." Krista tried to sound cheerful. "What can I do for you?"

He immediately went into a reprimanding speech, exactly like Pauline had just described. Taking Krista to task over Saturday's work party—holding her personally responsible. "You might be city manager, but you are not authorized to make major financial decisions without approval from the council or leadership team."

"Excuse me." Krista held up her hands to stop his tirade. "You're jumping to conclusions, Winston. You need to get your facts straight."

"And I saw you and Conner on Friday afternoon," he continued in a sharp tone. "Having coffee at Cupid's. And on city time too. You were obviously collaborating with him about the abatement contract. Besides allowing unauthorized work, you showed favoritism. You didn't even consider the other contractors' bids before making a decision. I plan to take this to the council meeting tonight."

"Fine," she told him. "Do that. And you'll wind up looking like a fool."

He glared at her.

"Did it ever occur to you that Conner's abatement efforts on Saturday were a donation? A generous contribution to ensure that Christmasville could continue as planned?" Winston appeared to be speechless, which suited her fine. "Furthermore, as city manager I am allowed to have coffee with a citizen to discuss city-related projects *on* city time."

"Well, what about preferential treatment? You obviously showed favoritism to Conner's company."

"Do you imagine other construction companies would feel slighted to discover they'd been overlooked for the opportunity of donating their time and materials?"

"What about Owen Payne? Now that you've shown preference for Conner, where does that—"

"The actual abatement can be handled with bids as usual. Conner wasn't even that interested in that part. He was simply trying to help us out. In fact, he recommended Owen's company."

"Well, I—"

"While you're here, do you have a copy of that budget yet?" she asked him.

"I've been trying to work up a financial report for Christmasville," he retorted. "That's keeping me pretty busy."

"Then I suggest you get back to it." She picked up a packet of papers. "I have work to do. Good morning, Winston."

After he left, she went to talk to Pauline, relieved to hear that Conner was happy to donate his company's time. "That's wonderful," she told Pauline. "I didn't actually lie to Winston, but I did insinuate that the work could be donated."

"Well, it's all taken care of, so don't worry." She handed Krista a folder. "City Council agenda for tonight's meeting. It starts at seven."

"Thank you." Krista frowned. "I need to find a babysitter."

"What about Anna?"

"Would she be interested? On a school night?"

"She was just telling me she was trying to earn money for Christmas. I can find out and get back to you on it."

Krista smiled. "You really are a treasure, Pauline." She wanted to hug the older woman but knew that wouldn't look very professional. Instead she just thanked her—again.

By the end of the workday, Anna had gladly agreed to babysit Emily. Naturally, Emily was thrilled at the prospect of spending the evening with a "cool teenager." She was dropped off a little before seven and, after an inconsequential council meeting that the mayor adjourned earlier than usual, Krista got Anna home before nine. Although she'd appreciated Anna's availability at such late notice, it wasn't very convenient to drag Emily in her pajamas to get Anna home. Especially on a school night.

"Bye, Anna," Emily called out sleepily. "And thanks for helping me—on *you-know-what*." She giggled.

"Well, just keep working on it," Anna told her. "We can go over it again on Thanksgiving if you want."

"Yeah. I'll bring it with me. Good idea."

Krista watched as Anna went into a handsome two-story house. It was hard to see too much of it in the dark, but it looked like Edwardian style. And like the house where Emily's friend Laurel lived, this was in the historic neighborhood too.

"What is it that you and Anna are working on?" Krista asked as she drove them toward home.

"It's a secret." Emily giggled. "Something for Christmas. Please, don't ask me. That would spoil everything."

"Oh?" Krista nodded knowingly. "I see." Emily had been making Krista homemade Christmas presents for the past several years. But she didn't usually start this early. It was a good reminder that it was about time to ask Emily what she wanted for Christmas. But not tonight. It was already past her bedtime.

To Krista's relief, the short week passed quickly, and on Thursday afternoon, she and Emily were parking in front of a handsome two-story farmhouse with a wraparound porch. Opposite the house was a classic red barn. "What a pretty place," she said as Pauline opened the door. "It's absolutely picture-perfect."

"Thank you." Pauline took the hot casserole of baked yams. "We enjoy it."

As Krista removed her coat, she introduced Pauline to her daughter.

"I'm very pleased to meet you," Pauline told Emily.

"Where do you keep your goats, Mrs. Harris?" Emily asked politely.

"Oh, you don't have to be that formal," Pauline told Emily. "Why don't you—"

"*Grandma.*" Anna popped around the corner with a grin. "You should just call her *Grandma*, Emily."

"Sure." Pauline smiled. "That's a good idea."

"And the goats are out in the pasture behind the barn," Anna told Emily. "Can we go see them, Grandma?"

"Of course. The turkey won't be done for at least an hour so there's plenty of time."

Krista wasn't sure why she felt nervous as she followed Pauline through the house, but she suspected it was related to meeting Conner's wife. She'd enjoyed getting acquainted with Conner during the past two weeks, maybe even too much. It would feel strange to meet his significant other. And yet she wanted to know her.

"This is my daughter, Julia," Pauline told Krista as they went into the kitchen.

"Pleased to meet you." Krista shook the tall brunette's hand. She definitely resembled her brother.

"And that's my husband, Kyle." Julia pointed to a nearby family room where the guys were intently watching a football game. "I guess you can meet him later. The game's in the last quarter. And one team is Kyle's alma mater and the other team is Conner's. I think they even have some bets on the table."

Krista looked around the old-fashioned kitchen, which smelled delightful. "I love this kitchen," she told Pauline. "Those must be the original cabinets and the sink and countertops too. It's charming."

"Mom's nagged Dad to redo this kitchen ever since they

moved here," Julia said. "But Dad always claimed he was too busy with work."

"And now that he's retired, he's still too busy." Pauline put the yams on the back of the stove, then set Krista up snapping off the ends of the green beans.

"All those goats keep him occupied." Julia returned to peeling potatoes.

"But I don't really care anymore," Pauline said. "This kitchen has grown on me. Now I just call it *vintage*."

"Speaking of vintage, have you guys seen the Christmas House lately?" Julia asked. "It's really coming along. I stopped by there yesterday to drop off some pillows and rugs and things, and it looks awesome."

"Julia has a shop in town," Pauline told Krista. "She's donating some things." She turned to Julia. "I haven't been by since the moving day. Maybe I'll pop in tomorrow. Dad's been there almost every day—painting—but he said he's nearly done now."

"Emily got to see it last week. She told me that it's been painted red and green on the outside. She said it looks just like a real Christmas House." Krista frowned slightly as she snapped a bean. "I haven't seen it myself, but red and green sounds a little, well, *Christmassy*."

"It's not the traditional Christmas colors," Julia explained. "Not bright crimson and kelly green. The body of the house is a dark sage green and the trim is creamy white, with burgundy shutters and door. I wasn't sure about it myself when Dad told me. The owner of the paint store donated the paint, and his wife selected the color palette, so no one wanted to complain. But when I saw the finished house, I was pleasantly surprised. It's actually quite charming."

"Well, I can't wait to see it." Pauline opened the oven to baste the turkey. "I read in the paper that there's an open house on Sunday. Do you think the house will be ready by then, Julia?"

"I sure hope so. I plan to spend most of tomorrow there. I'm working with my designer friend. We hope to get it all staged and set up by Saturday. Feel free to pop in if you want, Mom. You too, Krista." Julia dropped a potato into a pot. "That way you can have a sneak peek and miss the crowds."

"How does the contest actually work?" Pauline asked. "All I know is that contestants write essays. But when does it happen?"

"The deadline for the essay contest is December seventh," Julia told her.

"That's just a week away," Krista said. "And they only just moved the house."

"Yes, but the contest has been in the paper for the past several weeks. People have been sending in essays—five hundred words or less—explaining why they want to win the house."

"Who reads all those essays?" Krista asked.

"The newspaper staff reads them initially," Julia explained. "To sift them down." She laughed. "Beth admitted that a lot of them were pretty lame but provided some good laughs. After they eliminate most of the essays, there's a committee of twelve people from all over the community who will read and vote. And, of course, the essay writers are anonymous."

"That seems fair." Pauline put the finishing touches on a veggie platter. "But how do they do that?"

"The entrants include their contact information in a sealed envelope. So the judges don't know whose they're reading. According to Beth Seymour, they've already received hundreds of entries. She thinks there might be nearly a thousand before they close it."

"Interesting." Krista was actually more interested in where Conner's wife was hiding out just now. Surely, she'd come with Conner and Anna today. Maybe she was watching the football game. She snapped a bean in half. "When I first heard about the Christmas House contest, I wondered why they didn't just raffle the house. That could've raised money for Christmasville's general fund."

"And that would've pleased our CFO." Pauline winked at her. "But to be honest, I think the essay contest sounds like more fun. Housing is such an issue in this town, I'm sure there are plenty of people who could write a good essay about—" She was interrupted by a rousing yell from the family room, where the sports fans were obviously still glued to the TV. "Must be a good game," she said. "Probably almost over."

"Is Conner's wife here?" Krista asked, then instantly regretted it. She could tell by Pauline's and Julia's faces that it was the wrong thing to say. But she couldn't take it back.

"Conner's wife . . ." Pauline reached for a dish towel. "I didn't realize you didn't know."

"Didn't know?"

"Brianna passed away almost six years ago," Julia told Krista. "Lymphoma."

"Oh, I'm so sorry to hear that." Krista felt her cheeks grow warm. "I didn't know. I just assumed . . . well, he wears a wedding ring."

"Yes, we've encouraged him to remove the ring," Pauline said. "But he says he does it for Anna's sake. She was only eight when her mom died. The same age as Emily now. And she was worried that they would forget her mom. Conner wears the ring as a reminder that they won't."

"That's really sweet." Krista snapped the last bean just as Anna and Emily came back into the house.

"The goats are so cute," Emily told them. "I wish I could have one for a pet, Mama. Do you think we could—"

"We live in an apartment," Krista reminded her, "with a no pets policy."

"Come on, Emily," Anna called. "Come see my room." And just like that, they were off.

"Does Anna live here?" Krista asked Pauline.

"No, but we've always kept a room for her. She stays here a lot during the summertime—when Conner is working."

The football game ended and the women all laughed to learn that Conner, the loser of the bet, was paying off his brother-in-law by running to the creek and back. Before long, they were all seated in the dining room, bowing their heads as Roy Harris said a blessing.

As they visited and ate, Krista realized how much at home she felt with this family. And although it felt good, it was disturbing. She remembered the last time she'd felt at home with a family on Thanksgiving. She'd been just a little older than Emily, living with a new foster family in Phoenix. A really nice family. Or so she'd thought. However, it had all unraveled shortly before Christmas when the father was accused of something terrible with one of the older foster kids. She shuddered inwardly to think of it now.

After dinner, Anna and Emily disappeared upstairs to "finish something" and Krista offered to help clean up, but Pauline wouldn't allow it. "Why don't you give Krista a tour of the farm?" she asked Conner. "I'll bet she'd like to see the goats."

"Would you?" Conner asked.

"I'll admit I'm curious."

"Then let's do it."

She followed him to the foyer. "But I have to confess I was actually thankful for our tiny apartment's no pets policy when Emily asked to bring one home."

"Well, the kids are pretty cute. You might be tempted to adopt one after all." He chuckled, helping her into her coat. He pointed down at her black suede pumps. "Do you want to borrow some boots? It can be pretty mucky out there."

"I think I'm okay." She smiled. The truth was she didn't want to lose the bit of height the heels provided. But once they got outside, walking through the muddy farmyard, she realized it was a mistake. Still, she didn't plan to admit it. "This farm is so charming," she said as he opened the barn door. "It must've been delightful to grow up here. Like a storybook."

"My parents only bought this place ten years ago. Anna and I actually live in their old house in town." He opened a bin and scooped out some grain into a coffee can. "This is to feed the goats." He handed it to her then led her through the barn, opening another door in back. "Just give the can a shake and they'll come running."

Before she knew it, she was surrounded by some lively goats and kids in a variety of colors. The eager animals clambered about her like a bunch of puppies. And there was no denying they were adorable. No wonder Emily had loved it. Krista had never experienced anything like this. She followed Conner's instructions to hold grain in the palm of her hand, watching the funny animals gobble it down. But soon there were more goats and kids, eagerly pushing and prodding until she started to topple over backward. Conner caught her from falling into the mud.

"Oh my." She looked into his startled eyes. "Thank you."

"Here, let me help you." He took the remaining grain and poured it into a nearby plastic trough. "They can get a little rowdy when it comes to food."

They stood close together, watching the goats rush the trough, pushing and shoving to get their share. Krista's good shoes were coated in mud and her long black coat was splattered a bit too, but she didn't even care. She couldn't remember feeling this carefree before—at least not for a long, long time. She turned to Conner. "I know you've been through some hard times, but you and your family seem truly blessed to me."

"We have a lot to be thankful for." He paused as a particularly pushy goat nudged against her. With one arm around her, he kept her from tumbling. "Even in the hard times, well, it's a good reminder that God allows the rain to fall on the just and the unjust. We've all had our troubles."

"That's true. And I like to think our troubles make us stronger," she declared.

"And perhaps more empathetic too."

She looked up into his eyes, still enjoying the feel of him holding her tight. "I hope that's true. I'd like to be more empathetic." Suddenly uncomfortable with their closeness, she started to step back. "But sometimes I think I focus more on trying to appear strong. I guess that's a by-product of being independent for so long." She attempted a weak smile. "Makes a girl tough to stand on her own two feet."

He grinned. "I like tough girls."

She felt herself blushing. "I'm sure it's been helpful to have your family around. Having their support through your hard times." She tried not to feel envious—she really was glad for him . . . and for them.

"I can't disagree with you there." He looked deeply into

her eyes now, with such an intensity she felt slightly breath-less. "And I can't deny that my life is getting better all the time, Krista. Hopefully yours is too." His smile warmed her throughout.

"I hope you're right," she murmured. Then, feeling very self-conscious, she pulled away from his embrace, giving her full attention to the feeding frenzy that was about to end. She wondered if Conner and his family fully realized how good they'd had it all these years. Living in such a magical place, having each other to lean on . . . Perhaps they were used to it by now—although she doubted that they took it for granted.

· 10 ·

K rista had never attended a live Christmas parade before, but because Emily was so insistent, she knew
she had no choice. So with a thermal cup of coffee in
hand, and dressed in her new thermal underwear and down
parka, she walked with Emily, who was even more bundled
up, toward town.

"This is so exciting." Emily straightened her mittens as they
quickly walked toward Main Street. "Tonight we have to go
to the grand opening."

Krista mumbled yes, but her heart said no. Everything she'd
heard about these last two weeks was related to Christmasville. Even though she'd pretended to have on blinders while
going from the elevator to the front entrance of City Hall, it
was impossible not to see the transformation going on. And,
sure, she knew the people were having fun doing it. But all
this trouble, this expense, just for a holiday that would quickly
come and go . . . well, she was almost inclined to agree with
Winston the Scrooge. Was it really worth it?

Krista couldn't deny that the parade was charming, but it
was also cold. According to the weather report on the radio,

it was thirty-three degrees today and would drop to the mid-twenties tonight! But still no snow in the forecast. The parade finally ended with Santa riding in an old-fashioned wagon that was pulled by some majestic Clydesdale horses.

"Where are Santa's reindeer?" Emily asked as she shoved the candy she'd gleaned from the parade participants into her pocket.

"Probably vacationing in Palm Springs," Krista told her. "Ready to go home and get warm?"

"Wait." Emily waved to someone just crossing the street. "There's Laurel. Can I tell her hi, Mama?"

Krista nodded with reluctance. She was cold and ready to go home but waited as Laurel and Emily greeted each other, visiting like chatterboxes.

"Mama," Emily called. "Can I go to Laurel's house?"

"May I," Krista corrected.

"May I?" Emily smiled hopefully. "Laurel invited *me*. I didn't even ask."

Jessie approached Krista with a warm smile. "We'd love to have Emily this afternoon. But I have to run a couple of errands first. Could you drop her off around one?"

"Please, Mama," Emily begged.

Krista couldn't refuse her. And at least this would get her off the hook for putting up their artificial Christmas tree. Emily had insisted today was the day to do it, but Krista didn't even think the bulky tree would fit in their tiny living room. She wished it would accidentally disappear—like the missing box of ornaments—but she didn't dare get rid of it.

To further distract Emily from putting up the inconvenient tree, Krista offered to take her to Comet's for lunch. Of course, the drive-in restaurant, like everything else in town, was decorated to the nines with fifties-style lights and ornaments.

"It looks so pretty. Don't you just love Christmas?" Emily said as they pulled in.

Krista feigned enthusiasm she didn't feel. Mostly she felt she would love Christmas when it was behind her. January couldn't come soon enough.

After Krista dropped Emily off, she saw Julia removing a box from a van parked in the driveway next door. "Hey, Krista," Julia called out. "Come see the house."

Krista hadn't really intended to visit the Christmas House, but didn't see a gracious way of avoiding it now. It wasn't that she was opposed to the general idea of giving away a house, but it bothered her that Emily was so enamored with the whole thing. Still, she was curious.

"I like the exterior," she told Julia as she joined her on the little front porch. "Is this part new? I don't recall this when they were moving it."

"Yes, Conner felt it needed a porch. And a pair of hickory rockers are coming later today."

"The colors are really attractive." Krista ran her hand over the recently painted shutter. "It's Christmassy, but not garish."

"Come see the inside." Julia balanced the box as she opened the door. "It's nearly set up."

Krista went in and gazed around in wonder. "I can't believe this is the same house that was being moved down the street just two weeks ago. Everything looks so good."

"It's been a real rush job." Julia set the box on a cream-colored sofa. "But everyone has helped."

"It's so beautiful." Krista looked over the gleaming hardwood floors and comfortable-looking furnishings. "And yet it's homey and welcoming. It even smells good." It was a delightful combination of cinnamon, vanilla, and pine.

"We continued the sage-green, cream, and burgundy color scheme in here." Julia removed a lamp shade from the box, setting it on a pretty lamp base.

Krista went over to the kitchen, which was open to the living room. Sage-green cabinets with glass knobs, white marble countertops, and vintage-look appliances only added to the overall charm. "It's quaint but looks efficient." She ran her hand over the cream-colored farm sink. "It's perfect. And it even has an island."

Julia led her around the rest of the house, showing her the two smaller bedrooms, complete with attractive furnishings. One was set up as a bedroom, one as a handsome office. "And this is the guest bath. Small but fresh and pretty."

"Very nice." Krista ran her hand over more white marble.

"This is the master suite." Julia opened up the door to a slightly bigger bedroom with pale green walls, fluffy white bedding, and a burgundy easy chair.

"Very inviting," Krista said. She peeked into the master bath, which had a color scheme similar to the other bath. "It's all just perfect. Whoever wins this house will be very lucky."

"And the color scheme is such a great backdrop for Christmas decorations. Doesn't it make you want to start decorating?" Julia said with enthusiasm.

Krista wasn't too sure about that but nodded anyway.

"The designer is coming over later to do that. She'll put up lights and garlands and a noble fir tree in front of the big living room window. It'll be absolutely gorgeous."

"I'll bet this place will be like Grand Central Station tomorrow," Krista said as she walked back through the living room, pausing to admire the stone fireplace. "Thanks for letting me have a sneak peek today. It's truly beautiful."

"Thanks. It's been a real community project."

Krista opened the front door but was reluctant to leave.

"I'll probably see you at the ceremony tonight," Julia called from the kitchen. "Be sure to dress warmly. I hear it's going to be cold. But no snow forecasted yet."

"Emily and I will be wearing lots of layers," Krista called from the front porch, thanking her again as she closed the door. Then she stood there for a moment, imagining what it might feel like to relax in a rocker here, to live in a home like this. And for some unexplainable reason her eyes filled with tears at the thought. She hurried to her car, hoping that no one would see her. Really, it was silly to get emotional over a house. What was wrong with her?

Whatever it was continued later that evening. The opening ceremony was complete with old-fashioned carolers who led the crowd in singing, a dance company that performed the Sugar Plum Fairy, and the high school marching band that played some lively Christmas songs. Finally Mr. and Mrs. Claus made their appearance in a horse-drawn sleigh—then ceremoniously pulled the switch to light the enormous tree— and the crowd cheered wildly. Krista was glad that it was dark out as she wiped a stray tear.

"We officially open Christmasville to the public!" Santa (aka Mayor Barry) announced. "We have something for everyone. The ice rink will be open until nine o'clock tonight. And the missus and I hope you will come visit us in City Hall. Mrs. Claus has cookies fresh out of the oven in her Christmas kitchen."

"And hot cocoa and coffee," Mrs. Claus added. Krista wondered if Emily recognized her principal.

"My elves will be busy in my workshop," Santa continued.

"And you can find me putting my feet up in my cozy den—ready to listen to all my little friends' Christmas wishes. You can even visit my reindeer in their corral behind City Hall. We have all sorts of fun and games lined up. So I wish you, one and all, a very merry evening."

As Krista led Emily—or maybe Emily was leading her—through all the trimmings and trappings of Christmasville, she thought that perhaps this festival was a good thing after all. It was fun to feed a reindeer a carrot. And even more fun to greet their new friends here and there. Some, like Krista and Emily, were simply strolling about and enjoying the festivities. Others were actually in costume and at work. Conner and Anna, dressed like elves, were busily "making toys" in Santa's workshop. Although they were careful to remain in character, Conner did pause from hammering on a wooden wagon to wink at Krista. All in all, Christmasville appeared to be a real success. And Krista could see how having much of it indoors was a real plus. Even with the heat turned off, it was warmer than being outside.

"When do we get to be elves?" Emily asked as they exited City Hall.

"I'll have to check with Mrs. Morgan," Krista told her. "But I think next Saturday will be our first time."

"And we'll wear costumes like Anna had on tonight?"

"That's right."

"Oh, Mama," Emily gushed. "I just love Christmasville. And I love Winter Hill too. Thank you for moving us here."

"I'm glad you love it, Em. I love it too."

Emily looked up in surprise. "Really? You love it? Christmasville too?"

"I think so." Krista felt slightly teary again. "The whole thing has grown on me."

"Does that mean you love Christmas too?"

Krista sighed as she unlocked the car. "It means I'm working on it, Em. But you'll have to be patient with me, okay?"

"Okay," Emily said cheerfully.

As Krista drove them the short distance home, she wondered how it was possible that this quirky little town had made such major changes in her thinking in only two weeks. It was nothing short of miraculous. But she was glad for it. For Emily's sake, she was very, very glad. Tomorrow they would put up a Christmas tree. But not that silly artificial tree. Krista would take Emily to the Christmas tree lot and they would pick out a real tree. Not a huge one, but one that would fit into their little apartment.

· 11 ·

Krista couldn't remember the last time she'd been in such good spirits—*in December*. But as the first week of her most dreaded month peacefully passed, she felt like she'd conquered her anti-Christmas demons. She and Emily had gotten a real tree that smelled delightful and was now decorated with all new ornaments that they'd purchased at Mrs. Claus's Christmas Shoppe on Sunday afternoon. And after a week of doing a bit of lunch-hour shopping, Krista even had placed several wrapped gifts beneath the tree. Naturally, Emily was ecstatic over these new developments.

Emily had also been acting rather mysterious. Krista suspected that Anna Harris was helping Emily with some kind of homemade Christmas present because Emily had been in contact with her off and on throughout the week. Not that Krista minded Anna picking Emily up after school now and then. Handy since the high school was only a few blocks down the street. Krista had even offered to hire the teenager to watch Emily after school, since she knew Anna wanted to earn money for Christmas, but Anna had mysteriously refused payment. She claimed that she was hanging with Emily "for the fun of it." Still, it helped to break up Emily's week of after-school care in the school's gymnasium. And perhaps Anna would agree to be hired, with pay, to watch Emily during Christmas break. That would sure make life easier.

"Anna wants me to spend the night at her house tonight," Emily told Krista on Friday morning. "Is that okay?"

"She wants you to spend the night?" Krista frowned. "Why?"

"It's a secret." Emily pulled her backpack out of the car. "Is that okay?"

Krista shrugged. "I guess so."

"Great. And she'll pick me up after school today." Emily hopped back into the car to kiss Krista goodbye. "Thanks."

"Don't forget we're on elf duty tomorrow afternoon," Krista reminded her. "We're supposed to report at noon."

Emily nodded. "I know. I can't wait." She blew another kiss then pulled on her backpack and ran up the steps to her school.

As Krista drove to City Hall, she wondered what she'd do on a Friday night by herself. If the apartment had a bathtub, she'd indulge in a bubble bath. But it only had a shower stall. An ugly one that motivated her to keep her eyes closed while shower-ing. Maybe she could watch an old movie or read a book.

As Krista went through the decorated first floor to the el-evator, she was actually looking forward to Christmasville this weekend. The festivities were only on the weekends until the last weekend before Christmas. Then it would be open every night, and Krista had agreed to work several four-hour shifts, along with Emily, between now and then.

When Krista reached the elevator, Winston was just getting in. And he didn't look pleased to see her. Probably because she'd been dogging him all week to get her a copy of the budget, and she wasn't ready to back down. But first she greeted him. "Since you've had a hard time getting the budget to me, I asked Pauline to look around to see if someone else still has a copy," she told him as they went up. "Perhaps someone on the budget committee might loan me their—"

"There is no budget committee," Winston told her.

"No committee?" She frowned. "So only the mayor and the City Council review the budget then?"

"That's right." The doors opened and Winston stepped out in front of her.

Krista followed him out. "Well, maybe the council or mayor can loan me a copy."

"As a matter of fact, my assistant already dropped a budget report by your office, Ms. Galloway." He sounded a bit smug. "It's probably on your desk right now."

"Well, thank you." She smiled stiffly. "I look forward to going over it." As she continued to her office, she was determined not to let Winston get to her. Sure, he was irritating and had rather poor social skills, but if he was a good accountant, who was she to complain?

"Good morning," Pauline greeted her. "You'll be pleased to hear we finally got a budget report. In fact, you've got two. One from our CFO and one from the mayor. They're on your desk."

"When it rains it pours." Krista unbuttoned her coat.

"You probably won't have time to review it today. Your schedule is pretty full."

"I suppose I could take it home with me."

"Or save it for next week, since it doesn't look terribly busy." Pauline opened her date book, going over the meetings scheduled for the day. She'd just finished when the phone rang. "It's for you." Her brows arched with interest. "It's my son."

"Oh, okay." Krista pointed to her office. "I'll take it in there." Curious as to why Conner was calling, she answered her phone in her usual business tone.

"Sorry to bother you at work," he said. "But I wanted to ask you something."

"It's no bother." She slipped off her coat, laying it on her desk. "Does this have to do with Emily spending the night at your house tonight? I know she and Anna are working on something that's top secret. I suspect Anna is helping Emily make me a present. But I'm trying not to act overly curious."

"As a matter of fact, it's related to that. I wondered if, since Anna will be with Emily tonight . . . well, perhaps you'd want to spend the evening with me."

"With you?" Krista sat down.

"Yes, I thought we could get some dinner and, well, I don't know if you like ice-skating or not, but I thought it might be fun to pay a visit to the Christmasville ice rink."

"I've never ice-skated in my life."

"Well, I'm a pretty decent skater. Maybe I can give you a lesson."

"Or maybe you could peel me off the ice when I fall on my face."

He laughed. "I'll do my best to make sure that doesn't happen. And you're such a petite lady, it probably won't be too difficult to keep you from falling."

"Then I accept, Conner. I'd love to learn to ice-skate."

"Then it's a date," he said. "I'll pick you up around six if that's okay."

"That's great. I'm looking forward to it." She couldn't believe it as she hung up. Conner Harris had just asked her on a date.

A real date. She hadn't been on a date in years . . . not since Garth, but she didn't want to think about that now.

Dinner at Rudolph's proved both enjoyable and difficult. Being with Conner was fun, and it was interesting to hear about his wife, Brianna. She sounded like a genuinely good person—a good wife, a good mother—and then she got sick. He explained how Anna had been only six when her mother was diagnosed with stage four Hodgkin's lymphoma. "It had already spread into her lungs. She spent the next eighteen months in and out of treatments, but we finally realized the cancer was winning. Six months later, we lost her."

"I'm so sorry."

"It's been six years now." He rubbed his left-hand ring finger, where the wedding band was visibly missing. "I still miss her, but I have Anna." He smiled. "And a pretty full life. I think I've pretty much moved on."

They chatted some more, just light conversation, but then he asked her about Emily's father and she knew it was her turn to be forthcoming . . . and that was when it got difficult. She wanted to be honest. He deserved that much. But hopefully she could keep it brief.

"It's been about three years since it fell apart. At the time, I blamed everything on the other woman. But in the long run, I realized that Garth and I were a complete mismatch. We never should've married." She sighed. "But then I wouldn't have Emily. And I honestly don't know what I'd do without her."

"I know what you mean. A child motivates you to keep moving forward."

She nodded. "My relationship with Garth started in college. Although I had a good scholarship, I worked part-time to cover my dorm and expenses. As a result, I felt sort of lost and disconnected from the usual student activities. But Garth always popped in just when I needed a break from the monotony. He had friends and a life, and being with him made me feel connected. When he proposed, I thought we'd live happily ever after. But it turned out that Garth preferred fun to domesticity. After seven years, I found out about his girlfriend and we parted ways. Not long after the split, I learned that he'd been cheating on me almost from the beginning of our relationship. It was just how he was wired."

"I'm sorry." Conner slowly shook his head. "That must've hurt."

"Yeah, it was pretty painful." She looked down at her plate. "It made me feel like I wasn't good enough."

"*He* wasn't good enough."

She nodded, eager to wrap this up. "Garth remarried about a year ago, and they moved to Atlanta. I actually feel kind of sorry for his new wife. I'm afraid history will repeat itself with her."

"Probably." He pushed his empty plate aside. "Is he involved with Emily at all?"

She described the situation. "Unfortunately, he's been somewhat negligent. I'll admit that it's been easier to have him out of the picture, but I'm sure that Emily wonders. For her sake, I wish her father were part of her life." She sighed. "But there's not much I can do about it, and I'm not holding my breath."

"Well, if it's any consolation, Emily seems to be a happy, healthy, well-adjusted child. I think she'll be just fine." He smiled. "Anna is quite taken with her. She's enjoyed helping her on the, uh, the project." He made a zip-the-lips gesture, tossing the key.

"I know, I know. The big secret. Did you know that Anna has offered to babysit Emily during Christmas break? I hope that's okay."

"Of course."

"Emily is thrilled."

They visited congenially during dessert, and then Conner announced it was time to hit the ice. "Not literally," he said as he helped her into her down parka.

"I'm praying there'll be no broken bones," she confessed as they went outside.

"I'm sure we'll be fine." He smiled down at her. "You're so little that even if you do fall, it'll probably be a delicate landing."

"You must believe the old adage, 'The bigger they are, the harder they fall.'"

"Something like that." He pointed toward the tall, brightly lit Christmas tree in the town square. "I figured we could just walk to the rink, if you don't mind."

"Not at all. The town looks so pretty at night." She looked around. "I haven't been much of a Christmas fan . . . *ever*. But lately, I mean since moving here, I've been changing. Trying to change."

"Emily told us that your birthday is on Christmas Eve, Krista. And that you had a lot of disappointments as a child, and no real family. I think it's understandable that you'd have some reservations at Christmastime. Sort of like holiday PTSD."

"Holiday PTSD?" she repeated. "I think that pretty much sums it up."

"But you're in recovery now." He linked his arm into hers

as they walked through the town square. "And you're about to go ice-skating."

By the time Conner led Krista onto the ice rink, she was glad she'd worn two sets of thermal underwear beneath her jeans. Not only did that offer more padding in the event of a tumble, it was actually keeping her fairly warm. Her legs wobbled as she attempted to keep the blades of her skates moving in a straight line, and she felt like a klutz. Not wanting to splatter herself all over the ice as young skaters skillfully swooped past her, she clung even tighter to Conner's arm.

"Try to relax," he told her as he guided her along the edge of the rink. "Don't think about it too much. Just go with the flow. And lean on me as much as you like."

After a couple of awkward loops around the rink, with no falls, she finally started to relax. "You're a good teacher," she told him as they started to increase speed. But she was still clinging tightly to his arm.

"You're a good student." He smiled down at her. "I thought you'd be a fast learner."

After about an hour, Krista suspected she could probably skate without his assistance, but she didn't want to let go of his arm. She liked the feeling of being that close to him. And being a novice skater provided a good excuse.

"We should probably take a cocoa break." He gracefully guided her out the exit, still supporting her with one arm. "Your ankles might need a rest."

"And you might want to regain the feeling in your arm." She chuckled as she released him. "I'm afraid I've cut off your blood supply with my death grip."

"Not at all."

They spotted Julia and Kyle at a picnic table and went over to join them. The four of them conversed easily, like old friends, as they consumed cocoa and cookies. Krista felt completely at home with these people—so much so that she almost wanted to pinch herself. It seemed almost too good to be real. Maybe it wasn't.

After warming themselves by the fire-pit, they returned to the rink, and this time, Krista proved to herself that she really could skate unassisted. It felt amazing to glide along without help. Almost like flying. Her confidence was steadily building and she realized she actually liked skating. Then Conner even showed her how to skate backward. She moved at a snail's pace, but at least she was moving.

"I think I've become a real ice-skating fan," she told him as he linked her arm for a couple's skate. "This is a lot more fun than I expected. I'll bet it's good exercise too. I can't wait to bring Emily. She's been begging me to take her skating, but I keep putting her off. I think I'll bring her here tomorrow."

"We should go together," he told her. "Anna is a fabulous skater. I'm sure she'd love to teach Emily."

"That'd probably be better than me teaching her." Krista chuckled. "And knowing Emily, she'll probably be skating circles around me in no time."

"So it's a date? You and I, bringing the girls here tomorrow?"

"It'll have to be in the evening, Conner. Emily and I are on elf duty until five."

So it was set. Another date! Okay, maybe it wasn't a real date. Just two parents taking their girls skating. Or maybe it *was* a date. Or maybe it didn't matter. What did matter was getting to spend more time with Conner.

Krista couldn't remember a better weekend—ever. In fact, it was practically magical. So much so that it was almost scary. How could something this wonderful last? It was as if she'd been put under a Christmasville spell. Ice-skating with Conner, playing elves with Emily. More ice-skating on Saturday night. Going to church with all the Harris family on Sunday. A Christmasville caroling hayride on Sunday evening. It was like living in a storybook. But like all good things, Krista knew it would probably end. Hopefully not badly.

On Monday morning, Krista was somewhat grateful to get back to her nine-to-five routine, and first on her agenda was to go over the city budget. But as she reached for the recently printed document that Winston had finally managed to get to her, she noticed something. It looked slightly thicker than the mayor's copy sitting right next to it. Interesting. She did a quick check on the page count to discover Winston's report had more pages. Curious over the difference, she flipped through both documents one page at a time to discover they were not identical. What did this mean?

She took her time now, going over both spreadsheets line by line and highlighting the discrepancies. The only conclusion she could make was the doc from Winston had been adjusted. But why? Was there a logical explanation? Or was Winston trying to cover up something? Krista had recently read an article that suggested embezzlement in general was on the rise. Could he possibly be guilty of this sort of fraud? That was a serious accusation and not something she planned to leap lightly into. Not without concrete evidence.

She called Pauline into her office. She was still trying to make up her mind how much to divulge, but she decided that of all the city staffers, Pauline was probably the most reliable and trustworthy and perhaps the most knowledgeable. Due to retire in a year, she'd worked for the city longer than anyone else. Including Winston.

"Have a seat," Krista said slowly. "I need to talk to you."

"You look troubled." Pauline pulled a chair closer to the desk. "Is something wrong?"

"I'm not sure . . . Maybe." Krista tried to gather her thoughts.

Pauline leaned forward. "Is this about Conner?"

Krista blinked in surprise. "Conner?"

Pauline looked slightly embarrassed. "Sorry. But I know you've been spending time together." She smiled. "Which I happen to think is quite nice. And, don't say you heard it from me, but he does too."

Krista felt her cheeks warm. "Well, I have certainly enjoyed his company, but no, this isn't about him." She pointed to the spreadsheets lying open on her desk. "Something isn't right here. These don't match up."

"What do you mean?" Pauline leaned forward.

Krista quickly explained the discrepancies, pointing some

lines out specifically and asking how they could differ so much. "You've worked for the city a long time, Pauline. Do you think it's possible that Winston is doctoring the books?"

"You mean embezzlement?"

"I hate to say that. But something isn't right."

"It's a well-known fact that no one likes reading the annual financial reports. I know I never have," Pauline admitted. "But it's not part of my job description. But I've heard the mayor complain and I seriously doubt he reads them thoroughly."

"Yes. And there's no budget committee, which concerns me."

"The city councilors are volunteers with full-time jobs and busy lives. I'd be surprised if they went over these docs with a fine-toothed comb."

Krista sighed. "Don't you think that leaves plenty of opportunity?"

Pauline frowned. "What do we do?"

"Well, I certainly don't want to accuse him." Krista drummed her fingers on the desk. "How about if we request the reports from previous years. I could tell him I'm doing an analysis."

"How would that help?"

"Well, if he's been doctoring the books, he might get nervous. He might make excuses and try to delay it. That alone is a flag."

"And?" Pauline adjusted her glasses, peering more closely at the reports.

"What would you recommend?" Krista asked her.

Pauline's expression grew firm. "An investigation."

"With the police?" Krista grimaced.

"If Winston has embezzled funds, it's a serious crime, Krista. Not only would that be stealing from the City of Winter Hill, it's robbing decent, honest, tax-paying citizens."

"I know. But if he's innocent, it could blow up in our faces. And I'm the new kid on the block." Krista stared down at the spreadsheets. Her gut told her that something was definitely not right, but was she ready to stick her neck out?

"You need to speak to the mayor, Krista. *Today.* In the meantime, I'll play sleuth. I'll go to Winston's office and tell him you want the budget reports for the last five years, and I'll say that you need them ASAP. He has to have them on file—it's the law. I'll ask for his hard docs with the assurance that I'll copy the spreadsheets myself and get the originals directly back to him. Then I'll watch how he reacts." Her brows arched slightly. "I'm pretty good at reading people."

Krista agreed, so Pauline went one way and Krista the other. With the spreadsheets in hand, she went straight to Mayor Barry's office. Finding him working on his computer, she apologized for the interruption. "It's urgent."

"Come in. Come in." He smiled, then noticing her serious demeanor asked what was wrong. As she quickly explained, his brow grew furrowed. "Do you really think Winston could be stealing from the city?"

"I honestly don't know. That's just the worst-case scenario." She told him about the article she'd recently read. "Given the circumstances, it's probably a legitimate concern." She confided that Pauline was doing some sleuthing right now. "She suggested we contact the police. Although I'm not sure about that."

"Let's not jump the gun, Krista." He pursed his lips.

"Trust me, I don't want to. But I don't want to ignore this either."

"No, no, of course not. But how can the police be of any help?"

"Well, I assume they'd check his bank statements and look for any kind of evidence."

"Oh my . . . oh my." He rubbed his chin. "You realize this could get very messy, Krista. What if you're wrong?"

"That's what concerns me. I don't want to be sued for libel." And she didn't dare voice the words, but she realized she could be risking her job.

"And to have something this negative exposed right in the middle of Christmasville." He slowly stood, shaking his head. "It will be a black eye for the city—for sure. Whether Winston is guilty, or if he's falsely accused and innocent."

"So what do we do?" Krista felt her stomach tying into a knot.

Mayor Barry was pacing back and forth behind his desk now. "We probably should call an emergency council meeting. But then it's out there. It's impossible to keep something like this under wraps. Word leaks out and then it's an even bigger problem."

"Small-town gossip." She sighed.

"Why don't you just confront Winston?"

"Seriously? Just walk into his office and ask if he's been embezzling?" Krista shook her head. "That could blow up as easily as anything. He already doesn't like me."

"Then I'll ask him."

Krista didn't particularly like the sound of that either.

"Yes, that's probably the best plan. Straightforward and forthright." The mayor nodded firmly. "Yes, I should handle this. After all, I'm the mayor. And don't worry, Krista, I won't make an actual accusation. I'll simply raise the flag. I'll give Winston the chance to explain why these reports are different."

"Well, if you think that's the best route."

"I do." He picked up the spreadsheets. "Mind if I take these?"

"No. But, please, don't hand them over to him. We might need them as evidence later on."

The mayor picked up the docs and headed straight for the finance department. As much as Krista wanted to witness the scene, she didn't want to interfere. After all, she and Winston were already at odds. And she'd only been on the job three weeks. Far too soon to get involved in a sticky situation like this. She hurried back to her department, silently praying that Mayor Barry's visit would go well. Dismayed that Pauline wasn't back yet, Krista went into her office and, just like the mayor, began to pace back and forth.

"Well, that was interesting." Pauline closed the door behind her with a grim expression.

"Tell me everything." Krista leaned against her desk.

"For starters, I didn't care for Winston's reaction when I asked for the financial reports. He started giving the same excuses as before. But I stood my ground, reminding him that an auditor could show up and demand them just like that." She snapped her fingers. "I think the word *auditor* got his attention. So he reluctantly retrieved the spreadsheets, but insisted I remain in his department to copy them—with his assistant supervising. So that's what I was doing when the mayor showed up." Pauline sank into a chair with a weary sigh.

"What happened?" Krista asked.

"Well, I'm sure the mayor didn't intend to make it sound like he did. But I have to warn you, Krista, it did not sound good."

"What happened?"

"Mayor Barry began the conversation by divulging to Winston that you were concerned about discrepancies in the budget."

"Oh, no." Krista stood up. "The mayor said *that*?"

"He told Winston you'd asked him to look into it."

"I didn't think he was going to bring me into it." Krista was pacing again.

"I suspect he was trying to maintain Winston's confidence, Krista."

"How so?"

"By making it appear as though you were the one investigating him."

"That's just great." Krista controlled herself from rolling her eyes. "As if Winston doesn't already have it out for me. I don't understand why Mayor Barry would give him more ammunition."

"I guess the mayor is playing good cop, bad cop." Pauline's expression suggested she didn't approve either.

"And I'm the bad cop." Krista groaned.

"Winston, as you can imagine, claimed complete innocence and indignation."

"And he'd probably like my head on a plate by now." Pauline nodded.

"I think it's time to talk to the city attorney." Krista sighed as she reached for her phone.

By ten thirty, Krista, the mayor, and Byron were meeting in the conference room, with Pauline taking notes. Although the mayor appeared inclined to believe in Winston's claim of innocence, Byron, after looking over the two budget reports, came to the same conclusion as Krista. "Something is definitely wrong," he told them. "And the prudent thing to do at this point is to give Winston administrative leave while an internal investigation is conducted. His assistant should be placed on leave as well. Just in case she's involved. Or even if she's not."

"Do we contact the police?" Mayor Barry asked with a creased brow.

"You could do that. Or else you can hire someone to conduct a private investigation. I can make some recommendations."

"What about the council?" Krista asked. "Should they be informed?"

He nodded to Mayor Barry. "That's up to you."

"I wish we could keep a lid on this," the mayor told him. "At least until after Christmasville wraps up."

"I totally agree." Krista looked at Byron. "I'd like to recommend you supervise an internal investigation," she told him. "That way we could be sure it's done properly and respectfully, and hopefully privately."

"Yes," Mayor Barry said quickly. "Let's keep this out of the public eye as well as the police department for the time being."

"Unless we find conclusive evidence," Byron assured them. "Then it'll be time to press criminal charges. It never pays to procrastinate. Once a flag's been raised, you give a criminal time to transfer funds or even leave the country."

"But if an investigator is watching him . . ." Krista really hated to be part of this. "Wouldn't any quick actions be noticed—then he could be caught red-handed?"

"Theoretically," Byron confirmed. "And in a way, it can be helpful. If Winston really is guilty, he'll probably act fast, which is why we need an investigator right now."

They talked awhile longer, finally agreeing that it would be best for Byron to engage an investigator before informing Winston and his assistant that they would be on paid administrative leave, starting today. "I'll say that they're being excused from work until a complete audit is performed," Byron told them.

"Good," the mayor said. "Perhaps you can make it seem like a little pre-holiday vacation."

"A vacation that could end up with jail time," Byron said wryly.

"Oh, I hope not." The mayor shook his head. "Maybe it's all just a silly mistake. And if it's not, well, I feel I'll need to blame myself. I've never given those budget reports my full attention. I doubt anyone has."

"One thing for sure," Krista declared, "I'm going to lobby for a council-appointed budget committee in the upcoming year. More citizen involvement will make it more difficult for something like this to happen again. I mean, if it's happened at all."

Things went from bad to worse as the week progressed. Neither Winston nor his assistant were pleased with their "pre-holiday vacation." Never mind that their leave of absence included full salary and benefits, unless and until they were proven guilty and culpable anyway. But the worst part was how quickly inaccurate gossip spread through town. Citizens seemed to immediately take Winston's side, claiming that after twenty-nine years of faithful service, he and his assistant had been unfairly fired by the new city manager. It didn't help that the few people she'd actually met felt she was too young and inexperienced for the position.

According to the mayor, who claimed he was attempting damage control, these false rumors were probably the work of Winston's wife. Val Palmer was one of those influential women who belonged to every civic club and committee, and regularly connected with half the people in town. Naturally, she'd circulated the faulty story, both in person and via social networking, in an effort to gain sympathy and protect her husband's reputation.

It wasn't long before Krista realized that most people in town genuinely believed that Krista, a power-hungry young outsider, was behind the whole mess. And it was rumored that she had only begun to "clean house" and that many city employees' jobs would be on the chopping block.

By Friday afternoon, Krista was emotionally exhausted. "I think Emily and I will lay low this weekend," she told Pauline as she turned off the lights in her office. "I just called Martha Morgan and asked her to find someone to replace us as volunteer elves at Christmasville tomorrow." She didn't mention that Martha had sounded glad to excuse them, as if she'd bought into the negative innuendo too.

"Are you sure it's a good idea to run and hide?" Pauline asked. "And won't Emily be disappointed?"

"She'd be even more disappointed if Val Palmer and her friends showed up and made a scene." Or threw rotten produce, she thought wryly as she pulled on her coat.

"Oh, dear. Well, I suppose that could happen. But I hate to think of you being held hostage by false accusations. You've done *nothing* wrong. And what about the festivities tomorrow night? The high school orchestra will be there, and the drama kids are performing scenes from *A Christmas Carol*. They're even announcing the winner of the Christmas House. Certainly, you and Emily won't want to miss all that fun. Not for the sake of small-minded gossip."

"I know you're right, Pauline. And I hate being so cowardly. But I also hate exposing Emily to this venom." She wrapped her wool scarf around her neck a couple of times, hiding part of her face. "But maybe there's a way I can go incognito. It'll be dark, so maybe no one will recognize me." She wanted to laugh, but couldn't quite pull it off.

"I just feel so sad that you've been portrayed like this. And that you feel the need to hide out all weekend." Pauline frowned. "But here's an idea, Krista. It's pizza and *White Christmas* night tonight."

"What?" Krista pulled her scarf back down.

"Just a funny old tradition we started when the kids were young. We'd bring home a couple of pizzas and watch the old *White Christmas* movie a week or so before Christmas. Why don't you and Emily join us tonight?"

"You know, I've never actually seen that movie."

"Then you must come! We'll expect you both around six."

Krista agreed and headed for the elevator, feeling hopeful. But as the elevator went down, her emotions went with it. How was she going to deal with this mess?

When the doors opened on the first floor, Winston was waiting to get in. "Winston," she said in surprise, trying to hide a rush of actual fear. "What are you doing here?"

"If it's any of your business, I came to pick up some of my personal things."

"Oh." She attempted a smile, keeping her hands over the door to keep it from closing. "Have you been enjoying your time off?"

He simply grunted.

"I wish I'd had a chance to speak to you earlier this week," she said. "I wanted you to know that I only expressed concern over discrepancies in the budget reports. I never meant to make any accusations. But it was protocol in the City of Phoenix to request an occasional audit if the numbers didn't add up."

"The numbers add up," he said woodenly.

"Well, that will be a huge relief to everyone. I'm sure it's all just a clerical error." She forced another smile. "In the meantime, I'd think you'd be enjoying the downtime. I know I would."

"Well, maybe you'll get yours." He pushed her hand away from the elevator door. "Excuse me."

Her knees felt slightly wobbly as she exited the elevator and watched the doors close. Perhaps she was reading more into it than she should, but the look in his eyes had felt seriously threatening. Oh, she didn't think he was planning anything truly diabolical, but it was clear he hated her. She'd honestly hoped to extend an olive branch . . . or at least try. But clearly, Winston Palmer wanted no part of it.

As she went to her car, she wondered what exactly he was planning to do in his office. Before she started the engine, she gave Byron a quick call and he promised to handle it.

· 13 ·

Naturally, Emily was thrilled at the news they were going to the Harris farm. She'd been somewhat aware of Krista's challenging week and had even heard some unkind words at school. More than anything else, Emily had sounded concerned that her mother was starting to hate Christmas again. Krista had tried to reassure her that the problems at City Hall were not related to Christmas or Christmasville, but Emily was thoroughly disappointed to learn they wouldn't be playing elves on Saturday.

"Can we still go to Christmasville tomorrow night?" Emily asked as Krista drove them to the Harris farm. "There's going to be lots of fun stuff—and they're going to give away the Christmas House. We don't want to miss that, Mama."

Part of her wanted to miss it completely, but another part wanted to give in. "Yes, we can still go to that," she conceded. Hopefully they wouldn't run into any haters there. Or perhaps the mayor's damage control methods would finally start working.

It was a pleasant distraction to pig out on pizza and watch the Christmas movie with the Harris family. And, of course,

Krista was always glad to see Conner. It was encouraging that he looked equally glad to see her. And when he invited her to help him fix a broken railing out on his parents' front porch, she eagerly accepted. Of course, once she got out there, she could see that he didn't really need help. But she held the rail in place while he did his repairs, watching his expertise as he used various tools to make the rickety rail solid again.

"I hear you've had a rough week," he said as he worked. "I wish I'd known. I would've made time to come cheer you up."

"Thanks. I hear you've been pretty busy trying to finish up a house in time for a family to get in before Christmas."

"Yes. The Garcias have been waiting a long time to get into their own home." He handed her the power tool to hold for him. "And if you think you and Emily are crowded, imagine a family of six in a space about as big as your apartment."

"Well, good for you for helping them. That's better than wasting your time on me."

He stood up straight. "I would not consider it a waste of time, Krista."

"I know you wouldn't." She smiled. "You're a good guy, Conner."

"Well, thank you." He tested the rail, seeing that it held firm. "That takes care of that." He pointed to the sky. "Now how about some stargazing?"

"Really?" She set the tool on a porch chair, then went down the steps and looked upward. "I don't see any stars tonight."

"That's because of the clouds."

"Oh, yes, the clouds. Emily is certain it's about to snow."

"I don't think so." He chuckled as he reached for her hand. "I obviously used the stars as an excuse to get you down here."

"Oh, you did?" She felt a happy rush of nerves. Was his excuse what she hoped it was?

Still holding her hand, he strolled toward the barn. "I was thinking about you a lot this week, Krista." He paused by the rail fence, gazing out across the pasture, illuminated by the moon filtering through the clouds.

"Despite my difficult week, I was actually thinking of you too," she confessed.

"I was going to ask you out tomorrow night, but Anna informed me that we need to be at the Christmasville celebration tomorrow. She plays flute in the high school orchestra and they're performing. But I thought maybe the four of us could go together."

"I'd love to go with you." She confessed her trepidation about being seen around town. "It's not that I'm afraid for my safety or anything like that, but it would be unpleasant to have a nasty encounter with Val Palmer or one of her friends—for Emily's sake."

"I happily volunteer to be your protector." He was just leaning down toward her. Looking earnestly into her eyes. Was he about to kiss her? She hoped so. But his intentions were cut short by the sounds of gleeful shouts coming from the house. They both turned in time to see Anna and Emily clomping down the porch steps, laughing as they raced to the barn.

"What's going on here?" Conner called out.

"Oh, I didn't know you were out here," Anna yelled back. "I'm going to show Emily the new baby goat."

"A new baby goat?" Krista said.

"That's right," Conner told her. "Let's go see it too." Soon they were all standing outside a stall, admiring the pint-sized kid that had been born just that morning.

"He's so tiny," Emily said as she knelt by the fuzzy brown-and-white critter. "I just want to take him home and keep him forever."

"Well, he needs his mother right now," Anna told her.

"And our apartment doesn't allow pets." Krista knelt beside Emily. "But I can understand why you'd like to keep him. He's awfully sweet." As she petted the kid's soft coat, she was thinking of Conner. Had he really been about to kiss her? Or had she simply imagined it? Although she'd been slightly relieved at the interruption, she was disappointed too. What would it be like to share a kiss with him? Would she ever find out?

As Conner led Krista and Emily toward the town square on Saturday night, Krista felt uneasy. She'd already told Conner her plan to keep a low profile tonight, and had even stuffed her hair into a wool hat and wound a muffler clear up to her nose. She told Emily it was because she was cold, but her hope was to avoid any recognition as they listened to the music and watched scenes from the old Dickens play. Due to Emily's height, they stood near the front, but off to one side where Krista felt concealed in the shadows. By the time Santa showed up at the end of the show, she had finally just begun to relax. It would soon be over and they could go home . . . and she could breathe easily.

Like the opening night of Christmasville, Mr. and Mrs. Claus made the grand finale appearance. After a few compliments on the evening's show, Mr. Claus told everyone that he had an important announcement to make. "As you know, tonight is the big night. We are going to announce the lucky winner of the delightful Christmas House," he said merrily. "You may have already heard that there were nearly a thousand entrants. I'm sure it wasn't easy for the judges to make their decision. Although I've been told the winning essay was *unanimously* chosen by the Christmas House Committee. And now I will share it with everyone." He cleared his throat and began to read:

The reason I hope I win the Christmas House is because I never lived in a real house before. But it is my dream to live in a real house. My mama says that's too big a dream for such a little girl. But she never lived in a real house either. She never even had a real family before because she lived in foster homes. Those are houses with parents who are not your parents. So they don't really love you. And that made her really sad. So now it's my big dream for Mama to have a real house. A real house with real love with her real family. That's me because I'm all that Mama has got.

If I win the Christmas House, my mama will see that Christmas is a really special time. She will see that big dreams really can come true. She thinks that Christmas is a sad time because she always had sad Christmases. And she always had sad birthdays too because her birthday is on Christmas Eve and when she was a little girl everyone was always so busy that they forgot her birthday. Now Mama pretends like she doesn't have a birthday at all. But I know she really does. So if I win the Christmas House, I will give it to my mama and it will be her best birthday and best Christmas present ever. That is why I want to win the Christmas House. Then me and Mama can live happily ever after. Thank you very much!

PS. I'm sorry this is not 500 words long. I am only 8 years old and 500 words is way too much for me to write.

Krista's knees felt like Jell-O and Emily was jumping up and down like a wild thing, shrieking loudly with joy as everyone around them clapped and cheered.

"We won, we won! Mama, we won."

"Will the writer of this essay please come up to the stage?" Mayor Barry said. "And her *mama* too?"

"Come on, Mama." Emily grabbed Krista's hand, tugging her forward. But Krista's feet wouldn't move and she felt like she was about to be sick. This was all wrong. Horribly, horribly wrong. Emily was about to get her heart broken, and Krista didn't think she could bear to see it. "Come on!" Emily tugged so hard that Krista went forward. Feeling like she was headed for the guillotine, she followed her oblivious daughter.

"Oh my! It's *you*?" Mayor Barry looked so shocked to see Krista that he appeared to momentarily forget he was Santa. "Well, ho, ho, ho." He welcomed them up with hesitation. "Who have we here?"

Emily ran straight to him, giving him a big hug. "Thank you so much, Santa," she shouted into the microphone he held in front of her. "I'm Emily Galloway. I'm the one who wrote that essay. And this is my mama. Her name is Krista Galloway. And I wanted to win the house for her."

"That's the city manager," someone yelled from the crowd. And now others began to murmur as well.

"Is that true?" The mayor seemed to be wearing his Santa hat again. "Are you the city manager of Winter Hill?"

"I—I am," she stammered. "And I had no idea that my

daughter had entered this contest. I honestly don't know what to—"

"We won, Mama!" Emily danced happily around the stage, still bubbling over with joy. "We won the Christmas House! We won!"

After she finally paused, the mayor continued. "Well, the committee unanimously selected your essay," he told Emily. "So it certainly looks like you won." He handed her a brass key. "Here is the key to your beautiful Christmas House. I offer you my best wishes and congratulations." He gave Krista a concerned look.

Emily clutched the key to her chest, still hopping and jumping for joy as some of the audience began to clap. But not all of them—the gesture didn't seem to hold much genuine enthusiasm. And Krista knew why. She truly wished the earth would open up just now and swallow her whole. Instead, she forced a smile and took Emily's hand. "I suppose we can sort this out later," she mumbled to the mayor, then quickly made her exit. Could life possibly get any worse?

Despite Conner's reassurance that everything would work out, Krista wanted to pack up her life and her daughter and return to Phoenix ASAP. She'd never been so humiliated— *ever*. And of course it would happen at Christmastime. Wasn't that just par for the course? Why had she ever believed she was over her holiday PTSD? Still, she kept these thoughts to herself as Conner and Anna drove them back to their apartment. Of course, Emily was convinced they would move into the Christmas House tonight, and, so far, Krista hadn't told her it was impossible. But she knew it was. She knew that house could never belong to her and Emily. Good grief, why hadn't the committee figured it out when they'd seen her daughter's name—Emily Galloway? After all, it was a small town. Everyone knew that Krista Galloway was a city employee and that she was clearly ineligible.

"We'll just get our pajamas and things for now," Emily was telling Anna in the backseat. "Then we'll go back to the Christmas House to sleep tonight. You have to come see it too, Anna. Since you helped me to enter the contest, you have to come see how nice it is."

At the apartment, Krista let Emily and Anna go inside, but remained out in front with Conner. "What am I going to do?" she asked him.

"Go enjoy Emily's house," he said simply. "She won it fair and square."

"But I work for the city," she reminded him. "I'm certain that makes me exempt from—"

"First of all, this wasn't a city project or a city contest," he pointed out. "Second of all, Emily is the one who entered—"

"With Anna's help."

"Anna already told me that Emily wrote the whole thing herself. It was Emily's idea. Anna simply helped with punctuation and to print it out and make sure it got entered into the contest on time. That's why she offered to babysit for free. It was their chance to work on it. But Anna confirmed that the words all belonged to Emily."

"Even so, Emily is a child. How can an eight-year-old win a house?"

"The committee obviously knew she was a child and yet they chose her, Krista."

"But you heard the crowd tonight. They feel it's unfair. And

I don't blame them. I feel like it's unfair too. I'm sure it's just a matter of time before someone comes to inform us it's a big mistake. And I've got to prepare Emily for that disappointment. Because I know they're going to take it away."

"*Who's* going to take it away?"

"I don't know for sure. But I just know—"

"Mama," Emily called through the still-open door. "Want me to get your stuff for you?"

"We can't—"

"Krista." He stopped her. "Don't ruin this for Emily."

"But why get her hopes up?"

"Because it's legit. The contest was part of Christmasville and the city does not own Christmasville. It's volunteers like my parents and me and my sister and her husband and hundreds of others. I'm sure the contest committee knew that Emily was your daughter—by the time they selected her, anyway. And they could've pulled the plug then, but they didn't. You and Emily won the house fair and square. You need to go enjoy it. And enjoy it with Emily. It's her gift to you. Don't take that away from her."

Krista wasn't convinced, but she was too weary to protest. "Well, I suppose one night won't hurt anything."

"That's right." He reached out to pull her toward him, giving her a nice solid hug. "It's going to be okay, Krista, I promise."

She looked up into his eyes, wondering how he could back such a claim, but she kept her doubts to herself.

"Christmas is a time for miracles," he said quietly. "Maybe it's time for yours." And then, to her total amazement, he leaned down to gently kiss her. Her heart fluttered with hope as she returned the kiss, interrupted by Emily's voice inside the apartment.

"Come on, Mama," she called out. "You need to pack your bag."

Conner smiled at her, patting her on the back. "You go get what you need for the night, and Anna and I will meet you over there."

Feeling slightly dazed and still questioning how this could've happened, Krista packed a few things, then she and Emily got into their little red car and drove over to the Christmas House. Conner and Anna were already there, waiting for them in front of the well-lit house. In addition to strings of white fairy lights outside, the interior lights were on as well. It was all very sweet and welcoming. Even the Christmas tree was lit. But Krista knew it was an illusion. By tomorrow, they would be booted out.

"Just relax and enjoy it," Conner told Krista.

"But I—"

"Remember you can only live one day at a time," he said quietly. "Just take this one night at a time for now, okay?"

She simply nodded. "Okay."

"This is so exciting," Anna told Emily as they all stood on the small porch. "Aren't you going to go inside?"

"Everything is so wonderful," Emily murmured. "Just like a dream that really came true." She ceremoniously handed the key to Krista. "You open the door to your new house. This is for you."

Krista's hand trembled as she unlocked and opened the door. It truly was beautiful. Even more spectacular than the last time she'd been here. But Krista knew it was too beautiful to be true. And it was heartbreaking to imagine the crushing disappointment Emily would experience when she discovered they couldn't keep the house.

Emily ran ahead of the rest of them, going inside and spinning around in the great room like a ballerina. "Do you believe dreams come true now, Mama? Do you?"

Krista couldn't speak, but her eyes were filled with tears.

"Oh, Mama, those must be tears of joy."

Without the heart to tell her the truth, Krista simply nodded. Her daughter would find out the truth soon enough.

· 14 ·

To her surprise, Krista slept well that night. Whether it was because of the fabulously comfortable bed or sheer exhaustion was unclear, but she felt a tinge better in the light of morning. And, just like last night, Emily's eyes were bright and shining as she bounced into the pretty master suite.

"We didn't pack any food," Krista told Emily as she finished brushing her teeth. "So we'll have to go—"

"There's food here. Remember the fruit basket on the counter? And I looked in the fridge and there are all kinds of really good things in there."

"Oh?" Krista frowned. "But maybe we shouldn't eat—"

"They're for us. And I already had a banana."

Krista sighed. Well, the worst the committee could do would be to bill them for what they consumed. Maybe it didn't matter. So she began to fix them a breakfast of farm-fresh eggs, gourmet bacon, sweet rolls, and juice. She even made a pot of delicious-smelling coffee.

"Does this feel like a dream, Mama?"

Krista nodded as she sipped her coffee. She didn't admit

that it felt like a dream that was about to knock them sideways, yet she felt certain that someone somewhere was working on a diabolical plan that would probably destroy Emily's faith in human kindness indefinitely. But how to prevent it?

"Emily," Krista said as they were putting the dishes into the sleek new dishwasher. "I want to be completely honest with you."

"Okay."

"There might be a problem." Krista closed the door then looked into Emily's eyes. "You see, I work for the city and I've read the city charter and—"

"What's that?"

"Oh, it's a big book of rules for the city and also for the employees."

"Okay." Emily went into the living room, sitting down by the Christmas tree.

"And I know there are rules that prohibit city employees from winning contests or profiting from the city in any way."

"What does that mean?" Emily looked worried.

"Remember how I told you I would be ineligible because I work for the city?"

"But what about me, Mama? I don't work for the city."

"But you're my daughter. That means they might take this house from us, honey."

Emily leaped to her feet. "They can't take it, Mama. I won it fair and square."

"I know you did." Krista felt her eyes filling with tears as she hugged Emily. "You wrote a beautiful essay. And in my heart, I will always think that you really did win this house— and that you gave it to me. Honestly, that's the very best part of this dream coming true." She choked slightly then looked into Emily's eyes, which were also filled with tears. "Don't you think so?"

"I—I don't know."

Krista hugged her again. "No matter what happens, Em, we have each other. That really is what matters. God will take care of us. No matter what. Right?"

"Yeah." Emily's voice was gruff with emotion. "But I really hope we can keep this house. It feels like it belongs to us."

"Tell you what." Krista wiped her eyes with the sleeve of her robe. "Let's just live like that for today. For today, this house is ours. Just yours and mine. And we will enjoy this time completely." She smiled. "Then we'll see what tomorrow brings. Okay?"

They spent the day completely enjoying the Christmas House. They made a fire in the fireplace. They ate the food. They watched a Christmas movie on the big TV that was cleverly hidden behind a pair of wooden shutters. Even when Conner called, inviting them to join him and Anna for dinner at Comet's, Krista declined. "We're spending the day together in our Christmas House," she explained. "Just Emily and me."

"That sounds nice," he said. "I'm glad to hear it."

"It's a good reminder of what Jesus said . . . that we can only live one day at a time," she told him, trying to sound brighter than she felt.

"Very true. So how do you like the house?"

"It's the most beautiful house in the world," she gushed. "We love it."

"That's nice to hear. My crew worked hard on it. Along with a lot of other people."

"Well, you did a fabulous job. Thank you."

"One reason I wanted to call was to tell you I'll be out

of town. I've got a big commercial project over in Spokane, something I started two years ago—back before I started this new housing development. Anyway, it should've been done by now, but we ran into some glitches with the EPA last fall, and there are still some loose ends to wrap up there. I expect to be gone all week. But I hope to see you when I get back."

"That'd be great."

"Oh, another thing. Have you heard from Beth Seymour? She said she was trying to reach you."

"There have been a few calls on my phone," she confessed, "but I've ignored them, letting them go to voice mail. You're the only one I answered."

"Then I'm honored. But if you feel like it, you should talk to Beth. I told her as much as I could. But she wants to do a story about you and Emily in your own words. And I can assure you it will be a positive story."

"Oh?" She considered this. "Well, then I guess I could call her back."

After she hung up she called Beth and, from the privacy of her bedroom, honestly answered her questions. "I'm sure that I was more shocked than anyone," she admitted. "And I fully expect that it was a mistake. But Emily worked so hard to do this—and she was over the moon about it. Well, I just couldn't stand to ruin it for her. Not just yet anyway. But I told her the truth. I warned her that someone will probably try to take the house away from us. And I'll understand completely if that happens. I know city employees are ineligible to win city contests."

"Well, it sounds as if you're handling it well. I was concerned for Emily's sake too. I've interviewed a number of people, and to be honest, the jury is still out. Some are convinced that the whole thing was rigged. Others feel that Emily won the house fair and square. I guess we'll just have to see how it plays out."

"I'm just hoping that vigilantes with pitchforks won't show up at our door and drive us out."

"Call me if they do. I'd love to get photos." Beth laughed. "Can I get your comment on the situation with Winston Palmer? It's all over town that you fired him. But if that's true, I'm sure you have your reasons."

"I don't think I'm free to comment on that yet," Krista told her. "The city attorney is handling that. Have you spoken to him?"

"Yes. He said 'no comment' too."

"Sorry. As soon as I get the green light, I'll be happy to tell you what's going on."

"Great. I'll hold you to that. In the meantime, I hope you and Emily enjoy that sweet little house. And I hope you get to keep it too."

Krista thanked her, and for the rest of the evening, she and Emily continued to enjoy their house. They had a nice little dinner, made popcorn, and even watched another Christmas movie. But as Krista tucked Emily into the sweet bedroom, she reminded her that it was in God's hands. "Even if we find ourselves back in our little apartment tomorrow, we still have each other." She kissed Emily. "That's more than enough for me."

On Monday morning, Krista dropped Emily at the Harris house so that Anna could babysit. Emily had suggested Anna come to the Christmas House, but Krista felt worried that someone like Val Palmer could show up and evict them. And even if it was just her overactive and negative imagination, Krista didn't want to risk that happening in her absence.

As soon as she got to her department, she could tell by Pauline's expression that all was not well. "I might as well get it out," Pauline said even before Krista removed her coat. "Winston Palmer is launching an inquisition on you. He's questioning you on the Christmas House and a couple of other trumped-up charges. He's in the conference room talking to the mayor and council right now."

"And I suppose I'm not welcome."

"You're not welcome, but I'm sure you have the legal right to be there."

Krista considered this. "No, I think I'll pass. Is Byron there?"

"Fortunately."

"That's good enough for me." She unbuttoned her coat.

"There's not much on the agenda this week," Pauline said. "But that's not unusual the week before Christmas."

"Maybe I'll take some time to go over the city charter again." Krista forced a smile as she removed her coat. "Review the rules on city employees winning city contests."

Pauline shook a finger at her. "It was not a city contest, Krista. It was a Christmasville contest."

"Yes, but the city is a sponsor of Christmasville."

Pauline frowned. "That's true."

"If you see Byron coming out of that meeting, could you tell him I'd like to meet with him?"

"You got it." Pauline nodded. "And, please, don't be too worried, Krista. I just know that it's all going to come out all right. All things work together for good . . . eventually."

Krista smiled stiffly. "I tried to tell Emily that too. Still, it's hard sometimes." She went into her office and sat down. She hated to give in to such discouragement, but this felt utterly hopeless. Right now, Winston was in the conference room, lobbying, she had no doubt, for her dismissal. What would she do if they told her to leave? She hadn't been here long enough to get a severance package. And she'd already tapped into her slim savings account just to make this move. Her rent at the apartment was paid to the end of the month, but how hard would it be to find a new job if she were fired? She bowed her head to pray, but the only words that came to her were "God's will be done." She repeated them again and again, then, determined not to give in to despair, opened the city charter and flipped to the employee section.

She'd just finished reading it for the third time when Byron came into her office. "Pauline said you wanted to see me." He sank into a chair with a discouraged expression.

"How did Winston's meeting go?" she asked tentatively.

"For you? Or for him?"

"Both." She took in a deep breath.

"Winston has nearly convinced the council that you're a power-hungry opportunist with no professional experience and no regard for Winter Hill. He claims that you wanted to get rid of him in order to get away with all sorts of things. Including winning that house, which he claims is a fraud."

"Yes, that figures." She sighed.

"He even had the gall to tell them that you hate Christmas and would like to put an end to Christmasville. He said you told him that when you first came."

"That is partially true. That's how I felt *then*. Not *now*." She frowned.

"He claims you used your innocent child as a guise to enter the contest, knowing full well that city employees were ineligible."

"Oh, that's ridiculous that I used Emily. But the ineligibility part—is that true?" She held up the charter. "I've read and reread this rather vague paragraph about city employees not profiting through remunerations, reimbursements, paybacks, contests, and so on. But would that include the Christmas House contest? It wasn't owned by the city, and Christmasville is not owned by the city."

"I'm working on interpreting these questions myself right now. I'll let you know what I find out as soon as I'm certain."

"So do you think Winston convinced everyone in there?" she asked. "Should I be packing my bags?"

"Too soon to say." He frowned. "But to be honest, it doesn't look good."

"And I assume you've found no evidence on Winston regarding the embezzlement suspicion."

"Nothing yet. But my guy is on it. Unfortunately, these things take time."

"Did the mayor stand up for me?"

"In a way he did. But he's trying to be diplomatic. And, naturally, he's concerned about how this casts a bad light on the city. A city employee winning that house . . . well, a lot of people feel pretty disgruntled over it."

She held up her hands. "I'd gladly surrender the house, Byron. If that's what they want, I'm more than willing. I'm only staying there for Emily's sake. I never entered that stupid contest. And I had no idea that Emily had. She never told me. I felt literally sick to my stomach when I heard she'd won." She couldn't even bring herself to confess how sickened she'd felt to have the whole town know about her pathetic childhood history. How completely humiliating! Perhaps the best thing would be to just quit now.

"Well, don't be too hasty, Krista. It might turn out to be perfectly legal."

"I don't even care if it does," she told him. "How can I live in a house—in a town—where it feels like everyone hates me?" She stood, going for her coat. "How can I possibly be city manager after losing the respect of the city?"

"Are you quitting?"

She was trying hard not to cry. "I'm not sure, Byron. I'm not usually one to give up so easily, but maybe I should quit. It would probably be for the best—for everyone. Mostly for my daughter. I can't imagine living here and subjecting her to this. It's hard enough for her to lose her dream house, but to have people treating her like some kind of juvenile criminal. Well, I can't put her through that." She opened her briefcase, shoving what few personal items she had into it. "I guess I am quitting. I'll send in an official notice later today. In the meantime, would you pass the word on to the mayor and council? I'm sure they'll be relieved." And before he could argue with her, she swooped up her coat and things and rushed out. To her relief, Pauline wasn't at her desk. Krista would have to explain it to her later.

She felt sick to her stomach as she drove over to the Harris house. There, she paid Anna generously for just two hours of babysitting. "I'm sorry, but we've had a change of plans. I won't need you to watch Emily during Christmas break."

"Is something wrong?" Anna asked with concern.

"I've quit my job," Krista said in a controlled tone. "It's for the best."

"Oh . . . okay." Anna nodded with a quizzical expression.

"Come on." Krista helped Emily into her parka. "We've got a lot to do."

"What do we have to do?" Emily asked with concern as they went outside.

As Krista drove, she explained her plan, trying to make it sound like they were embarking on a holiday adventure. "We're going to drive our new car to this lovely ski lodge," she said pleasantly, acting as if she'd already picked the place. "They'll have a gigantic Christmas tree and snow and all kinds of things. Maybe we'll learn how to ski. Won't that be fun?"

"What about our house? I thought we were going to have Christmas here—in our Christmas House."

"I know it's hard for you to understand." Krista kept her voice cheerful as they went inside the Christmas House to get their things and straighten it a bit. "But I don't think we get to keep this house, Emily."

"Why?"

"Remember I told you about my job with the city. Well, they had a meeting this morning and it looks like . . . well, I think the people in this town don't really want us here anymore. And it's just better for us to go *now*."

"But some people in this town want us here. Anna and Conner and the Harrises and my teacher and my BFF and—oh, Mama, why can't we stay?" Emily was starting to cry and Krista felt like joining her. Except she knew that wouldn't help.

"There are good people here who *do* like us," Krista reassured her as she packed her overnight bag. "But not everyone. And not the people in City Hall. That's where I had my job. You know that if I don't have a job, well, we don't have money to buy food or things we need. So we really have to go, honey. I need to look for a new job. But not until *after* Christmas. Don't worry, we'll have a nice Christmas up at the ski lodge. Just you and me." Krista blinked back tears as she picked up her bag. "But first we have to start packing up our apartment. Okay?"

As she helped Emily pack her bag, Krista ran a mental to-do list through her head. First of all, she'd call Pauline and tell her the news. Then she'd write a formal resignation letter—and she would put the Christmas House key inside of it. She'd make her letter as gracious and professional as possible and even ask Mayor Barry for a letter of recommendation.

She'd arrange for the U-Haul truck tomorrow—maybe one that could pull their little red car behind it. She'd give notice on the apartment and utilities. She and Emily would spend the next couple days repacking boxes. She'd pick up the moving truck by the end of the week and perhaps pay the twenty-something brothers next door to help them load it. By the weekend she and Emily would be out of Winter Hill for good.

· 15 ·

As hard as Krista tried to keep her bad feelings toward the city hidden inside, she knew they must've been seeping out. Emily was obviously more perceptive than Krista realized. And by Wednesday afternoon, her young daughter's negative comments were starting to concern her. Was Emily becoming as jaded as her mother?

"Winter Hill is a stupid old place," Emily declared as she dug out some pans from a low cupboard, handing them one by one to Krista.

"Why do you say that?" Krista set the frying pan into a box.

"This town is called Winter Hill, but it never even snowed here."

"That's true."

"And it's way too cold." She handed Krista a saucepan. "Last night, after I went to bed, it took forever for my feet to get warm."

Krista almost pointed out that the apartment's heating system wasn't too great, but thought better of it. "Yes, my feet were cold too. I guess we need some warmer socks."

"So all we get here is cold, cold, cold—*but no snow*." She

157

shook her head as she handed Krista a pie tin. "And even if it did snow, we don't have a backyard to build a snowman in. So what's the use?"

Krista sighed as she slid the tin down the side of the full box. "We could've had a backyard, but they tricked us."

"Tricked us?"

"Yeah, first they said I won the Christmas House and then they took it away. That wasn't fair. The people in Winter Hill are selfish and mean. Well, except for Anna and her family and my BFF and my teacher. But the rest of them are bad. Bad, bad, bad." She handed her a cake pan with a dark scowl.

"Oh, they're not all bad, Em." Krista thought about Conner as she closed the full box. She still hadn't heard from him this week, but she knew he was working out of town. Hopefully Pauline had tipped him off by now. "I'll admit that a few of them aren't too nice. But most of them really are good."

"If they're so good, why did they take the Christmas House away from me? Why did they make you quit your job? And why are we leaving?"

"It's a complicated story, Emily. But you just need to realize it's probably for the best. It'll turn out okay. We might have disappointments, but God never lets us down. Not in the end." Krista tried to believe this herself as she started to load another box. "Remember when I told you we were moving here? You were so upset about leaving Phoenix. And then we got here and you decided it was really great."

"Yeah, but now we're leaving *again*." Emily looked up with sad blue eyes. "I don't really *hate* Winter Hill, Mama. Even if it doesn't snow ever—" Her voice cracked with emotion. "It's just that I'm mad. Really, really mad."

Krista hugged her, holding her close. "The truth is I'm mad

too, Em. I know just how you feel." She let her go, looking into her eyes. "But I guess we'll just have to forgive them, won't we? Otherwise, we'll be stuck being mad forever."

Emily sniffed. "I don't think I can ever forgive them. Not the ones who took the house away from me. I just think that's mean and nasty. Just like the Grinch before he turned good. Santa Claus said—oh, I know he wasn't *really* Santa Claus because he's really the mayor and my principal is his wife and she was pretending to be Mrs. Claus. But the mayor said the Christmas House Committee picked my essay, and he said that I won. So how can they take my house away? How is that fair?"

"I don't know, honey." Krista didn't want to go over this again and again. What good did it do? She looked at her watch. "But I do know this—it's almost dinnertime and our kitchen is a disaster area. How about if we go to Comet's tonight?"

Emily agreed, but not with any real joy. And Krista felt oppressively sad as she drove them to the drive-in restaurant. She knew that Emily eventually needed to accept the realities of this world, but she was only eight. She had already been abandoned by her father . . . and now this. Wasn't that a big load for a little girl to bear? Krista felt certain she'd been through much harder things by that age, but she'd hoped for better for her child. Emily didn't deserve this!

By midmorning Friday, with the help of neighbors, Krista had the U-Haul truck completely packed. All she needed was to get her car onto the trailer behind the moving truck, and she and Emily would be on their way. Krista had already made a reservation at Moose Lodge, about four hours away, and the manager had even given her permission to park the U-Haul in an overflow parking lot until after Christmas.

As they stood outside the emptied apartment, Krista studied a YouTube video on her phone, trying to learn how to safely secure her car to the trailer. Halfway through the tutorial, her phone began to ring. Tempted to let the call go, she saw it was from Pauline and decided to answer. Especially since she still hadn't had a chance to speak to Conner.

"Oh, good," Pauline said quickly. "Where are you right now? Have you left yet?"

"In the parking lot outside the apartment." She smiled at Emily, tweaking the puff ball on her stocking cap. "We're all packed up and ready to go. We have reservations at Moose Lodge and—"

"Hold off a bit, will you?" Pauline sounded urgent.

"But if we leave now, we'll get there in daylight," Krista explained. "And I really don't want to drive this big truck after—"

"Well, then at least let me tell you the news. Or have you already heard?"

"I've been pretty busy, Pauline. I haven't heard any news."

"Can you hold for a moment?" Without waiting for an answer, Krista was placed on hold, listening to the peaceful instrumental music that City Hall hoped would pacify those waiting for assistance.

"Drat." Krista was tempted to hang up, but curious to hear "the news," she waited. She looked up at the lead-gray sky. Was it her imagination, or was it getting darker? Her watch said it was not quite noon.

"Okay, I'm back. You still there, Krista?"

"Yes. What's the news?"

Pauline proceeded to tell her that Byron Peters and his private investigator had collected solid proof that Winston had indeed done some serious embezzling. "He's been arrested and taken into custody, Krista. And his bail is set quite high."

"You're kidding." Krista sat down on the edge of the car trailer.

"Not in the least. Naturally, everyone was sort of in shock last night when it all transpired. Beth has been here all morning, getting the full story. I told her everything I know. I want this to make the news in a big way."

"I guess people have a right to know the truth." Emily sat down beside her, snuggling close to get warm.

"So, you can come back to your job now."

"Oh, I don't know." Krista felt torn. Part of her wanted to go back. But part of her still ached. She put her arm around Emily. "That doesn't really take care of everything, Pauline. There's still the question of city employees and ineligibility, you know?" She didn't want to go into details of the Christmas House again, not with Emily listening. "It's not only about Winston."

"But don't you see?" Pauline persisted. "Winston was using the Christmas House against you. It was his smoke screen. He wanted to take the focus from what he knew he'd done. He thought if he got you into hot water, he'd escape detection. But it didn't work."

"Seems like it worked to me. You heard about what the mayor and council said on Monday."

"Yes, but . . . hey, are you alone?"

Krista frowned in confusion. "Well, Emily is here with me."

"No one else? Yet?"

"What do you mean, *yet*?"

"Oh, I just—"

"Look, Mama." Emily tugged on Krista's parka sleeve. "There's Conner's big white pickup. Anna is with him."

"As a matter of fact, your son and granddaughter just pulled up."

"Oh good." Now Pauline hung up.

"Well, that was interesting." Krista pocketed her phone in time to see Conner parking beside the moving truck. But there were other vehicles pulling in as well and before long the whole apartment complex parking lot and the other side of the street quickly filled with cars too. Krista felt a slight rush of fear—had everyone come to run her out of town? But not Conner and Anna—they weren't like that.

"What's going on?" she asked Conner.

"We're here to take you home." He wrapped both Krista and Emily in a big bear hug. "Looks like you're ready."

"Home?" Krista asked as he released them.

"To the Christmas House," Anna declared.

"*What?*" Emily's eyes lit up.

Suddenly the mayor and his wife, all the council members, the Christmasville Committee, and members of the Chamber of Commerce gathered around. There were many others as well whom Krista didn't know. Even Beth was there, camera in hand and snapping photos.

"We are here to express our deepest apologies," Mayor Barry declared. "We hope that you will forgive us." He turned to Emily. "As you recall, Santa Claus told you that you were the winner of the Christmas House last week, but then certain things happened." He grimaced as his wife nudged him with her elbow. "Unfortunate things that we all deeply regret. But we are all here to officially declare that after a thorough and complete review, we have all determined *unanimously* that you, Emily Galloway, are the official winner of the Christmas House. Congratulations." He handed Emily the brass key again.

Krista was speechless—and slightly skeptical. Was this going to turn out like last time? It wasn't fair to put Emily through this again. But it was too late. Emily was already beaming. "Thank you, thank you," she cried out. "Thank all of you!"

Krista took the mayor aside as Emily continued to gush her gratefulness, leaping from one foot to the other with unbridled joy. "Are you sure?" Krista whispered to him. "I can't do this again. Not to my daughter. It will kill her."

"We had a big emergency meeting at City Hall just now." He nodded to the others all happily smiling. "Everyone agreed." He pointed to another car pulling up. "And that will be our city attorney and your assistant. Let Byron confirm it to you. He completed his legal research and gave me the first green light. But then I called the meeting and everyone agreed, Krista. Emily won that house fair and square. It's hers . . . and yours."

"It's true," Byron confirmed as he and Pauline joined the celebration. "Emily won the house. It's been determined that the Christmas House was never owned by the city and the contest was not run by the city. There are no ineligibilities. It's all legal and fair."

"And it will all be in tomorrow's paper," Beth told Krista. "Right next to the embezzlement news. So everyone in town will know the truth."

Conner wrapped an arm around Krista, giving her a warm squeeze as he sneaked her around to the other side of the U-Haul truck. "Remember I told you it would all work out." He leaned down to kiss her, taking his time—and leaving her breathless. "You need to trust me more." He grinned as he led her back to the excited crowd.

"And we've got plenty of hands to help you move your furnishings, the ones you don't need anyway, into a storage unit on my property." He patted the side of the moving truck. "That's great you're all packed up and ready to go—ready to go *home* to the Christmas House."

"Yes, yes!" Emily jumped up and down. "We're ready to go home! We're really, really ready."

Krista did not know what to say—she was literally speechless. So she turned to the happy crowd still gathered around her and simply murmured her thanks. But her eyes were filled with tears of genuine joy this time.

"You're welcome," the mayor said. "You're welcome—from everyone."

"You haven't just given us the Christmas House," she told them. "You've given us a home. Thank you. Thank you so much!" And now everyone cheered.

"Look, Mama!" Emily pointed upward with wide eyes. "It's snowing!"

And the crowd cheered even louder.

With around 250 books published and 7.5 million sold, **Melody Carlson** is one of the most prolific writers of our times. Writing primarily for women and teens, and in various genres, she has won numerous national awards—including the Rita, Gold Medallion, Carol Award, Christy, and two career achievement awards. Several of her novels have been optioned for film, with one scheduled as a Hallmark TV movie for summer 2019. Melody makes her home in the Pacific Northwest, where she lives with her husband near the Cascade Mountains. When not writing, Melody enjoys interior design, gardening, camping, and biking.

A Cozy Read for the Holiday,
FULL OF HOPE AND HEART

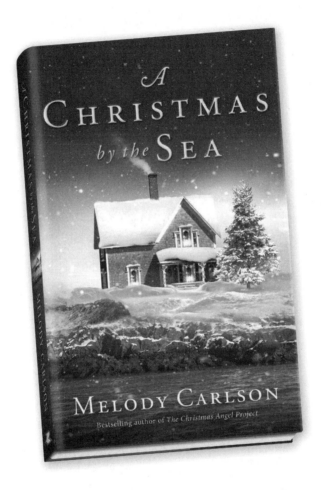

When a widow and her preteen son inherit a shabby but charming beach house in Maine, they move in with very different hopes. Can the Christmas season bring them the miracle they need?

More Christmas Adventures from
MELODY CARLSON

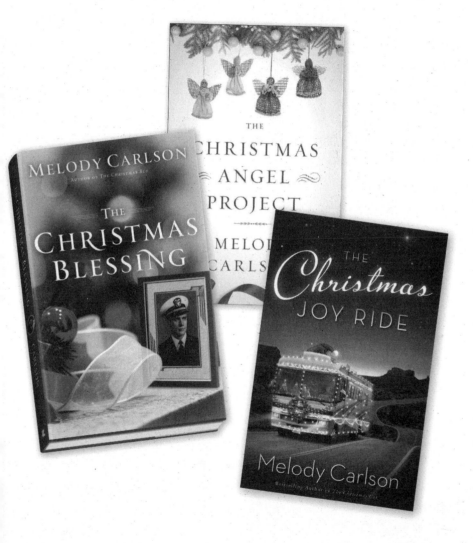

 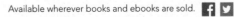

No One Is Too Old to Change Their Lives—
OR FIND A NEW LOVE

George Emerson doesn't want his predictable life to change, but free-spirited ex-hippie Willow West has other plans for him. They may soon discover that no one is too old to change their lives—or find love.

MEET
Melody

MelodyCarlson.com

f Melody Carlson